Izzy's
Pop Star
Plan

Izzy's Pop Star Plan

A Devo/Novel

ALEX MARESTAING

THOMAS NELSON
Since 1798

NASHVILLE   DALLAS   MEXICO CITY   RIO DE JANEIRO

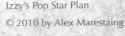

Published in Nashville, Tennessee, by Thomas Nelson. Thomas Nelson is a registered trademark of Thomas Nelson, Inc.

Thomas Nelson, Inc., titles may be purchased in bulk for educational, business, fund-raising, or sales promotional use. For information, please e-mail SpecialMarkets@ThomasNelson.com.

Photographs taken by Nicola Claire.

Library of Congress Control Number: 2010026200

Marestaing, Alex.
  Izzy's pop star plan / Alex Marestaing.
    p. cm. — (A Devo novel)
  Summary: Sixteen-year-old Izzy Baxter has wanted to become the world's next singing sensation since she was six years old, but now, just as she is competing on the hit television show "International Popstar Challenge," it seems that God has other plans for her.
  ISBN 978-1-4003-1654-0 (softcover)
  [1. Singing—Fiction. 2. Competition (Psychology)—Fiction. 3. Celebrity—Fiction. 4. Christian life--Fiction. 5. Blogs—Fiction.] I. Title.
  PZ7.M33525Iz 2010
  [Fic]—dc22

                                        2010026200

Printed in the United States of America

10 11 12 13 14 RRD 6 5 4 3 2 1

Mfr: RR Donnelley/Crawfordsville, IN/November 2010/PO#

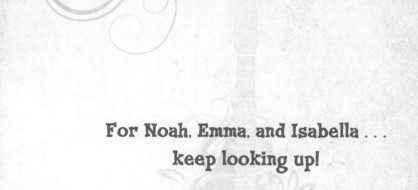

For Noah, Emma, and Isabella . . .
keep looking up!

Acknowledgments

My special thanks go out to:

Jenni Burke, Don Jacobson, and the entire D.C. Jacobson crew. Thanks for being the first ever "Izzy" fans.

Laura Minchew, MacKenzie Howard, Dan Lynch, and everyone else at Thomas Nelson who made these ideas come to life.

Nicola Claire, for fantastic photographs.

Chuck Booher, for so many Sundays of inspiration.

My precious three, Noah, Emma, and Isabella, for sacrificing so much "dad" time so that others could read "Izzy's" story.

Finally, to my wife, Margaretha, thanks for riding this roller coaster with me and always smiling along the way.

PART 1

Hollywood Home

I want you to know how much I really care,
And even though my heart's been hurting,
I'll be there.

"SING"—IZZY BAXTER

D@y 1: Hello World, It's Me!

Mood Meter: Terribly Talkative

I nervously twisted the mega-long sleeves of my sparkly, blue dress as I made my way up the steps toward the chanting crowd. As the lights dimmed and the band hit their opening chords, I could hear the twenty-thousand-plus fans going wild. "Izzy, Izzy, Izzy!" they screamed as I stepped out onto the stage. It was time for all my wildest pop star dreams to come true. It was time, time for . . . our church musical, and, well, it wasn't really like that at all.

To tell you the truth, there were probably only about sixty people in the audience that Sunday night. But hey, that's the way I saw it in my daydreaming, six-year-old head. Singing my very first solo, there in front of Hollywood Community Church, was a huge deal for me. The stage lights, the sound of my voice ringing out through the PA system, the applause afterward. I was hooked.

That night, I felt it for the first time, an unquenchable thirst for pop stardom. As I lay awake in my bed that night, I thought, *Izzy Baxter, you are destined to become a singing sensation*. I know, it sounds a little prideful, but hey, I was only six.

From that day on, I started studying pop stars like a mad scientist. I examined their every dance move and mimicked their vocal styles. My bedside table was stuffed with notes on everything from what Mindy Mars wore to the Grammys to Sean Benson's daily workout schedule. I even practiced smiling like them in the mirror. I was a hopeless pop-aholic.

When I was nine, I created a plan, the Pop Star Plan. The plan is made up of step-by-step directions on how to become, well, a pop star, of course.

When I first started writing the plan in my pink journal, I thought I'd be a star in no time. Boy, was I wrong. I've been following the plan like my life depended on it for the last five years, but haven't even come close to getting my big break yet.

But I'm not too worried about that, because something big is on the horizon, something *really* big. Well, if it actually happens, it'll be big. It has to do with a little audition tape I sent out last month.

More on that later, but for now, count yourself lucky. You are one of the chosen few who have been given the password to my

Unbelievable Blog. As your faithful blogger, I plan to keep you, my inner circle of friends, in the loop regarding my amazing pop star life.

If anything happens, you'll be the first to know, I promise.

My Heart

Commit to the LORD whatever you do, and your plans will succeed. (Proverbs 16:3)

I've changed a lot since I started writing the Pop Star Plan. For one thing, I've learned that even though I have this plan, God's the One who really knows what's going on. I mean, seriously, half the time I can't even figure out my math homework, let alone plan my entire existence. God's the only One who can make my biggest dreams come to life.

It's really important to commit all our plans and dreams to God. That means that we talk to Him about them, and let Him change our plans if He wants. When we give our dreams to Him, they can really fly.

Good Night, God

Lord, I give the Pop Star Plan to You. Add to it. Change it if You want. It's all Yours. Amen.

That's my prayer. What's yours?

L8R

---

2 COMMENTS:

Maddie said . . .
Watch out, world. Here comes Izzy Baxter! Woooo Hoooo!
Posted Monday, 9:32 p.m.

Pastor Ryan said . . .
Awesome! Can't wait to read the "way cool" and "off the wall" adventures of Izzy Baxter!
Posted Monday, 10:17 p.m.

Day 2: Fire Escape

Mood Meter: Thinking

Izzy's Unbelievable Blog is brought to you live from the fifteenth floor of the Alcove Apartments in Hollywood. I'm sitting on the rusty fire escape that's right outside my bedroom window. From this perch, I can see all the way to Warner Brothers Studios. That is, if there's no smog.

I started crawling out here a couple of years ago, after my mom died. My mom and I were the talkers of the family. We would sit and chat for hours. Sometimes when my dad and Anders, my big brother, were asleep, she would come into my room with a cup of hot chocolate, and we'd talk until, like, two in the morning. She would tell me about when she was a little girl, and I would tell her about, well, absolutely everything.

When she died, I felt like I had lost my best friend. I became like this crazy hermit from *Lord of the Rings* or something. I had NO ONE to talk to. I totally love my dad and all, but talking to him just isn't the same. He's more, like, quiet. I tell him things and he listens, but sometimes he doesn't really know what to say back. He'll get this serious look on his face, like he's trying to come up with something. Then he'll just hug me without saying a word.

Anyway, this one day I felt as if all the feelings swirling inside of me were going to cause my heart to explode. I didn't know where to go, so I crawled out onto the fire escape. I stared out at all the city lights and just began talking to God.

I had prayed before, at church and stuff, but this was different. I was talking to Him like a friend. I told Him everything, about how lonely I was without Mom, about how I couldn't really talk to my dad. I told Him mostly that I was really scared. When I crawled back into bed, I felt totally better. Nothing had changed in my life really, but I knew God had listened to me and that made all the difference in the world.

My Heart

I no longer call you servants, because a servant does not know his master's business. Instead, I have called you friends, for everything that I learned from my Father I have made known to you. (John 15:15)

Can you believe it? God, the Maker of the whole universe, calls us friends! Like the ultimate friend, He shares His heart with us and listens to what we have to say. So go ahead and tell Him your dreams and heartaches. He's totally listening.

Good Night, God

Hi, Lord, I just wanted to say thanks for calling me Your friend. I really appreciate it. Amen.

That's my prayer. What's yours?

L8R

---

1 COMMENT:

Maddie said . . .

I totally talk to God that way too!! Sometimes I set my Manga Bear timer for ten minutes, and then just start chatting away with God until the beep. It works for me!

Posted Tuesday, 9:07 p.m.

Day 3: Audition, Audition, and Audition Again

Mood Meter: Cautiously Hopeful

Brace yourself, because today I have some awesomely amazing, crazy cool news to tell you. Last month I sent this demo of me singing to the producers of *International Pop Star Challenge*. You know the show, the one with over seventy million viewers worldwide, the show that made Ryan Richards an overnight star, the show that "makes all your pop star dreams come true!" Well, this afternoon I got a phone call from none other than Giuseppe Rossi, one of the show's judges, and guess what? He wants me to audition for the show on Friday!

Even though he can be brutally honest on TV, he was nice on the phone. He explained that he and the other two judges had listened to my tape and thought I had potential, which I thought was pretty cool.

The only bummer is that he had been trying to call me for two weeks, AT THE WRONG NUMBER! Apparently, Anders, who wrote my phone number on the CD, used his notoriously messy printing, and the people at Quest Studios couldn't read it. So now I only have two days to pick a song to sing. Yikes!

I've been excited all day long, but I'm trying to calm myself down now. I don't want to get my hopes up too high. I've been to a gazillion auditions before (Pop Star Plan Rule #7: "Audition, audition, and audition again") and have been disappointed every time.

Failure is just part of the music business. I mean, Mellissa Smythe sang in New York subway stations for three years before Metropark Records signed her. Who knows? Maybe this will be my moment.

All I can do now is pick a song, practice it, and let God handle the rest.

My Heart

But those who hope in the L<small>ORD</small> *will renew their strength. They will soar on wings like eagles; they will run and not grow weary, they will walk and not be faint. (Isaiah 40:31)*

I think one of my problems is that I put too much hope into things rather than in God. I start thinking an audition or some new outfit will fill the emptiness I sometimes feel inside. I mean, it's fine to get excited about things, but when we put our *hope* in things rather than in God to solve our problems, we just end up disappointed. Put your hope in God instead, and you'll soar like an eagle.

Good Night, God

I'm putting my hope in You, Lord. You have this whole audition thing in Your hands. You know how much it means to me. Take my excitement and keep it safe in Your arms. Amen.

That's my prayer. What's yours?

L8R

---

2 COMMENTS:

Anders said . . .

Don't blame me, sis. Giuseppe is Italian, you know. He probably had a hard time reading English numbers. ☺

Posted Wednesday, 10:24 p.m.

Izzy said . . .

Nice try, bro. Thanks for helping me send the demo, though!

Posted Wednesday, 10:27 p.m.

D@y 4: Peace

Mood Meter: Nervous

"For the love of everything beautiful, let me go to sleep!" Mr. McGuire yelled from upstairs about fifteen minutes ago.

"Sorry," I squealed as I nervously stuffed my beat-up guitar into its case. He's probably not the only neighbor who's upset at me. I've been singing out here since eight this morning. Fourteen hours, three guitar strings, and four *entire* bags of sour ropes later, I'm finally satisfied.

Let me rewind a little. Last night, after I blogged, I got out my guitar and started messing around with some ideas. Pop Star Plan Rule #17 says, "Sing it like you mean it," so I was trying to come up with a song that I was crazy in love with. After looking at song lyrics online for about an hour, I started freaking out. "This is impossible!" I yelled.

Suddenly, it hit me. I had been trying to find the perfect song on my own. I hadn't even asked God for help yet. As I watched the fog roll in from the coast, I prayed, "God, this means more than a lot to me. Please help me find my song for Friday. I'm beyond desperate."

Not knowing what else to do, I just sat in the silence, watching the clouds come in from the beach. Then, out of the blue, I started humming this hymn, "How Can I Keep from Singing?" It was my mom's favorite. She used to sing it to me each night before I went to bed. She never stopped, even during that last year when she was really sick.

As I picked up my guitar, the words flooded back to me.

> *Through all the tumult and the strife*
> *I hear the music ringing;*
> *It finds an echo in my soul—*
> *How can I keep from singing?*

Right then and there I realized that God had given me my perfect song.

Today I spent the day "popping" it up a bit. It sounds more modern now, but the meaning is still there.

Anyway, I'm off to bed. Big day tomorrow!

My Heart

If any of you lacks wisdom, he should ask God, who gives generously to all without finding fault, and it will be given to him. (James 1:5)

Sometimes our problems stress us out so much that we forget to ask God for help. Next time that happens, take a deep breath and ask God what to do. He'll be more than glad to give you the answers you need. Really!

Good Night, God

Lord, please give me wisdom as I audition for the show. Help me totally rock tomorrow. Amen.

That's my prayer. What's yours?

L8R

---

3 COMMENTS:

Pastor Ryan said . . .
Awesome song choice, Iz. You should play it for us when you lead worship next week. You aren't too big of a pop star now to lead worship for us, are you?
Posted Thursday, 8:23 p.m.

Izzy said . . .
I'll have my people call your people. ☺
Posted Thursday, 8:59 p.m.

Stephanie said . . .
Hey! Ryan and I are your people.
Posted Thursday, 9:16 p.m.

Hey friends! Check out my first video blog at: www.izzyspopstarplan.com/videos and click on Day 4.

9

D@y 5: Oh Happy Day

Mood Meter: Blue Sky Kisses

Today was one of those stupendously, beyond birthday, happy days. It was one of those days that only comes around, let's see, about every GAZILLION years or so. It was audition day, and I have sooo much to tell you.

Where to begin? Where to begin? Okay, I got to Quest Studios at about nine in the morning. It's right down the street from my house, so I walked with my dad. A security guard checked for my name on a list and led us through the gates. When we got to studio 12, where the auditions were being held, there was this massive line stretching all the way around the building.

Standing there in the brutal California sun, I began to doubt my chances. There were auditions being held in twenty countries, and only one singer would be chosen from each. To make matters worse, Emily Elektra was standing in line in front of me. I'd seen her at a lot of my other auditions and knew that she was almost impossible to beat. She had been on Broadway before and had even appeared in a couple of movies.

By the time I reached the front of the line, I was a mess. Sweat had made my makeup run, and my hands were shaking.

"Miss Isabella Baxter, step into the studio, please," called one of the production assistants. It was showtime.

The first thing I saw when I stepped into the room was Japanese judge Aiko Mae. She smiled at me, like she always did to the contestants on the show. Next to her sat Marshall Phillips, the only American judge. At the end, arms crossed, sat the ultra hip Italian, Giuseppe Rossi.

Marshall asked me what song I would be singing. "It's a song my mom used to sing to me before she died," I explained. "I sing it to myself when I'm worried or scared. It kind of makes me feel better."

No one responded. They just watched as I got down on one knee and fiddled with the latches of my guitar case. Then I stood up, took a deep breath, and hit my opening chord.

As I got to the chorus, I pictured my mom singing along with me. I wasn't nervous anymore.

No storm can shake my inmost calm,
While to that refuge clinging;
Since Christ is Lord of heaven and earth,
How can I keep from singing?

When I was done, this scary silence hung over the room. I wasn't sure what to do. After a long pause, the Italian began to speak. "Your mother, you miss her, no?"

"Yes, very much," I answered simply, resisting the urge to bite my fingernails.

"Well, today you make her very proud," he said in this totally sincere tone.

I was stunned. Giuseppe Rossi, one of the toughest judges on the show, liked my performance. They all liked my performance. Aiko Mae was even wiping a couple of tears from her eyes.

I left the studio thinking, *I actually have a shot at this*. I gave the audition to God, and He came through. Now I *really* feel like singing.

My Heart

He will cover you with his feathers, and under his wings you
will find refuge; his faithfulness will be your shield and rampart.
(Psalm 91:4)

We have a God who is faithful. He will never, ever fail us. He will never, ever ditch us. Never, ever, ever, ever! No matter what.

Good Night, God

God, I needed You today, and You were there. Thanks for always being faithful. Amen.

That's my prayer. What's yours?

L8R

2 COMMENTS:

Maddie said . . .
UNBELIEVABLE!!! I wish I could've been there, Iz. See you tomorrow!!
Posted Friday, 11:08 p.m.

Stephanie said . . .
Call me, call me, call me! Ryan and I want to hear everything.
Posted Friday, 11:23 p.m.

Day 6: Maddie Mason

Mood Meter: Wishfully waiting

"Tell me everything!" screamed a voice in the middle of my perfectly wonderful dream this morning. I rubbed my eyes and squinted at the smiling figure looming over me. "What was Aiko like? Was she nice? Was Giuseppe as dreamy as he is on TV?"

It was none other than my early-bird best friend, Maddie Mason. We've been friends since kindergarten, and she lives a couple of apartments down from me. She's got stylish, short, black hair and is totally into fashion. When she's on her balcony and I'm on my fire escape, we can actually talk to each other, if we yell, that is. We used to do that all the time, until Mr. McGuire complained to our parents.

After that, we started talking by bird mail. My brother Anders, who is a total genius, rigged up this cool wire system between our rooms a few years back. Whenever we want to send a message to each other, we put a note in this cable car-type box, and it flies across like a bird. Bird mail! Now we mostly text, but it's still fun to bird mail things over every once in a while.

"It's six in the morning!" I said, throwing my pillow at her.

She smiled and began dragging me out of bed. "Your dad let me in. Time for LuLu's."

LuLu's is the coffee shop on the ground floor of my building. Whenever there's something BIG going on in one of our lives, Maddie and I go there for a double berry smoothie and some serious talking.

Today she listened to me talk about the audition forever. All of a sudden it dawned on me, "Mads, you were supposed to go to Santa Monica Pier with the youth group today!"

"Whatever. The pier will always be there."

"But you've been looking forward to that all week," I added, feeling a little guilty.

Then she got up and gave me this huge hug. "You're way more important than the beach."

By the typically huge Maddie smile on her face, I could tell she meant it.

My Heart

Greater love has no one than this, that he lay down his life for his friends. (John 15:13)

Maddie is always doing stuff like that. Once, during our freshman year, she even showed up fifteen minutes late for school because she was helping me find my runaway hamster, and then today she missed the beach trip. I mean, she doesn't just care about what's going on in *her* life. She really and truly is interested in mine as well. I guess true friends are like that.

Jesus models the truest form of friendship, though. He gave up His own life on the cross so that we could be forgiven of our sins and live forever. Now that's what I call the ultimate friend.

Do you have a best friend? Someone who cares about your dreams and heartaches? Are you being a good friend to them?

Good Night, God

Lord, help me love my friends like I love myself. Help me be a true friend. Amen.

That's my prayer. What's yours?

L8R

---

1 COMMENT:

Maddie said . . .
Thanks for the kind words. You're not such a bad bud yourself!
Posted Saturday, 10:31 p.m.

Day 7: A Couple Means Two, Right?

Mood Meter: Getting Restless

No, I haven't heard a thing from *International Pop Star Challenge* yet. Which I think is strange because at the studio, they told us that they would let the "chosen few" know in a couple of days. Well, I'm not a math whiz like Anders, but I know that it has been exactly a COUPLE of days since I auditioned. So far I've gotten zero calls, zero e-mails, zero texts, zilch. I don't know, maybe I'm taking the whole "couple" of days things too literally. Maybe they just meant that they'll let us know in, like, three or four days or something. The waiting has been driving me absolutely BANANAS!

Let's just say patience is not something I'm very good at. Anders says I'm about as patient as a fly. Hey, he's right. It's hard having patience sometimes, especially when you are waiting for something good to happen.

At least one good thing has happened out of this waiting business—a new song. I just came up with it today. It's not done yet, but the chorus goes something like:

> *When the storms come in and my dreams feel far,*
> *Lord, help me wait, help me wait in Your arms.*
> *When I hurt inside and can't see the stars,*
> *Lord, help me wait, help me wait in Your arms.*

I guess in the end this whole experience will teach me to trust God more.

I'll keep you posted.

My Heart

Be still, and know that I am God. (Psalm 46:10)

Pastor Ryan told us that the Hebrew word for "be still" in this verse means to "let go." So tonight I, Izzy Baxter, am going to try to let go of this whole *Pop Star Challenge* thing and trust that God has everything under control.

Are you waiting for God to do something? Relax, be still. God cares for you and knows exactly what you need. You're going to be just fine.

Good Night, God

Lord, help me be patient and trust You to keep my biggest dreams safe. Amen.

That's my prayer. What's yours?

L8R

---

3 COMMENTS:

Pastor Ryan said . . .
At least someone has been listening to my lessons!
Posted Sunday, 9:02 p.m.

James Baxter said . . .
Hang in there, baby.
Posted Sunday, 9:15 p.m.

Izzy said . . .
I'll try. Love you, Daddy.
Posted Sunday, 9:22 p.m.

Day 8: Seeds

Mood Meter: Green Gardening

Okay, following dear old Dad's advice, I've ditched my crazed phone babysitting and am moving on with my life and my music! Three hours of practice tonight! I didn't even realize how much time had gone by until Anders called me for dinner. Time flies when you're doing the things you love, and I love SINGING!

My mom used to tell me that I was born to sing like wild horses were meant to run. She was right. When I sing, I feel close to God and far away from everything that stresses me out. I practice every day, rain or shine.

Since I want to become a professional singer, I'm homeschooled. I usually take a lot of courses online, and my dad sets aside a couple of hours a day to help me with math when he's not setting up Web pages, which is what he does for a living. Doing school at home helps me keep up with my schoolwork when my audition schedule gets crazy. After school, I head into my dad's office, shut the door, and start singing away. I usually sing until around four, but sometimes, like today, I'll forget about the time and sing until dinnertime. I practice my scales, gear up for any auditions I have coming up, and spend some time on my guitar writing songs.

It's fun because the more I sing, the better I get. All that hard work is really paying off. Last June, I just missed getting a part as an orphan in a touring company of *Annie*.

A couple of weeks ago I decided to be as disciplined with my Bible and prayer times as I am with my music. I added this new rule to the Pop Star Plan: "Read the Bible and pray every day."

I figure if I can find time to sing each day, then I can find time to read and pray as well. So, as you've probably noticed, I've been including something I've learned from the Bible in each of my posts. That way you can keep up with what's going on with my heart, as well as my head.

My Heart

The one who sows to please his sinful nature, from that nature will reap destruction; the one who sows to please the Spirit, from the Spirit will reap eternal life. (Galatians 6:8)

If you plant a lot of "school seeds," you get better at school. If you plant a lot of "music seeds," you get better at music. But if you plant a lot of "God seeds" by praying, reading the Bible, and trying hard to do what God wants, then you'll grow the fruit of the Spirit, and that will make your life awesomely delicious (see Galatians 5:22–23 ☺).

Good Night, God

Lord, show me the best ways to use my time. Help me plant a lot of "God seeds" this year, so that good things can grow in my life. Amen.

That's my prayer. What's yours?

L8R

---

2 COMMENTS:

Maddie said . . .
I once stuck a potato in a cup of water, and it started growing hair.
    Does that count? ☺
Posted Monday, 10:48 p.m.

Izzy said . . .
LOL! Go to bed already. I can still see your light on.
Posted Monday, 10:51 p.m.

D@y 9: Fave Five

Mood Meter: Okay, I Guess

Four days, ten hours, and thirty-seven minutes, and STILL NO PHONE CALL! I've been pacing around the house with the phone in my hand all day. It's driving my family crazy. I'm totally freaking out!!!!

It's time for desperate measures. It's time for Fave Five.

Fave Five is this game I play whenever I'm totally stressed. I get out a piece of paper and write down five favorite things, you know, things I am totally into. By the time I'm done, I'm thinking about the things that make me happy instead of the things that make me miserable.

So here it goes. Izzy Baxter's Fave Five:

Coco (my stuffed monkey): I've had Coco since I was a little baby. He's kind of falling apart and starting to smell weird, but I'll always loooove him!!!

Old movies: Anders and I are crazy about them. We stayed up until midnight on Saturday watching *Singin' in the Rain*. It's this musical from the fifties. Man, that Gene Kelly can dance!

My green T-shirt: It has a camera with a strap painted on it. I look like a Hollywood tourist when I wear it. Pretty funny.

Long talks at LuLu's: Double berry smoothies + long talks = JOY

Singing in the car: Last week Anders and I were belting out an Elvis Presley song at a red light. I totally forgot that my dad had rolled down all the windows. When I looked up, a whole busload of elementary school kids were staring at us. I laughed until I cried.

I would have put the *International Pop Star Challenge* judges on the list this week, IF THEY HAD CALLED! But of course, they *didn't*, and so Giuseppe Rossi and his crew didn't make the cut.

My Heart

Whatever is true, whatever is noble, whatever is right, whatever is pure, whatever is lovely, whatever is admirable—if anything is excellent or praiseworthy—think about such things. (Philippians 4:8)

When we're down, we tend to focus on everything that is going *wrong* in our lives. When we do that, we just end up freaking out even more. God wants us to focus on everything that's *right*. Learn to do that, and you'll find a lot more sunny soul days.

Try making your own Fave Five list. Everything good in life comes from God, so be sure to thank Him when you're done.

Good Night, God

Lord, thanks that I can go to sleep tonight thinking about Coco, green T-shirts, and good friends. You must love me so much to give me all that stuff. Amen.

That's my prayer. What's yours?

L8R

---

3 COMMENTS:

Pastor Ryan said . . .
The Dodgers, spicy chicken wings, surfing, Nehemiah 8:10, and my
lovely bride.
Posted Tuesday, 7:17 p.m.

Anders said . . .
Perfect test scores, the Knowledge Channel, chocolate pretzels, German
shepherds, anything written by C. S. Lewis.
Posted Tuesday, 8:07 p.m.

Maddie said . . .
My pink and purple scarf, bare feet on warm sand, fashion, fashion,
fashion!!! Am I allowed to do that?? (Ha Ha)
Posted Tuesday, 9:11 p.m.

Day 10: What's Going on Here?

Mood Meter: Not Even Close to Happy

"The world's hottest pop star hopefuls are unveiled as International Pop Star Challenge *reveals next season's finalists. Meet them all on* Entertainment America's *morning show!"*

I heard that UNBELIEVABLY AWFUL news on TV about two hours ago.

You don't have to be a brain surgeon to understand this one. The *International Pop Star Challenge* finalists are going to be on *Entertainment America* tomorrow. *Entertainment America* is taped in New York. I am NOT in New York. I am 3,000 miles away in Hollywood. In fact, no one invited me to go to New York. That's because you have to be one of the *Pop Star Challenge* finalists to be invited to New York. I was NOT invited to New York; therefore, I am NOT going to be on *International Pop Star Challenge*.

My pop star career is ruined, absolutely ruined, before it even began. I have been crying nonstop for two hours now, and I won't be stopping anytime soon. I know that I've failed at auditions before, but this was different. The judges liked my song!

I thought for sure I had this one in the bag. I thought it was God's plan. Look at the way He gave me the song to sing at the audition and everything.

Sorry, guys, I can't even write anymore. I've got more important things to do, like sticking my head into my pillow and screaming.

2 COMMENTS:

Stephanie said . . .
I'm so, so, so, so sorry, Iz. Here's a verse for you.
"Do not fear, for I am with you; do not be dismayed, for I am your God. I
    will strengthen you and help you; I will uphold you with my
    righteous right hand" (Isaiah 41:10).
He's with you, Iz. Your tears are like prayers. He's hearing every single
    one. Ryan and I are praying for you, girl.
Posted Wednesday, 9:01 p.m.

Maddie said . . .
God, help my best bud. She really, really needs You right now. Amen.
I'll be over in the morning.
Posted Wednesday, 10:43 p.m.

Day 11: Ouch!

Mood Meter: Don't Even Ask

"Don't even think about turning on the TV!"

That's the text I got from Sabine, my other best friend, this morning. She was right. Watching *Entertainment America* would just confirm what I already knew. I wasn't going to be on *International Pop Star Challenge*, and someone else was. Why torture myself?

I couldn't help it, though. I tried to speed by the TV on my way to the kitchen, but the remote control drew me toward it like a tractor beam from one of those space movies Anders is obsessed with. I just HAD to find out who made it.

I plopped down on our tattered sofa and popped the switch. There, in painful high definition, sat next season's *International Pop Star Challenge*, contestants. They seemed so happy as they answered questions from the studio audience. Then the camera zoomed in on a face I recognized oh so well, Emily Elektra. Perfectly blonde Emily Elektra, who has beaten me out on my last five auditions. The same Emily Elektra who sings like an angel, but has the personality of a toothpick.

When she got up to sing, I turned off the TV and launched the remote across the room. It almost hit Anders in the face. Luckily, he had his head stuck in a book, so he didn't even notice.

I wished he had noticed, though, because I was mad. "Why would the judges choose some fake-named, makeup-smeared wannabe over me?" I wailed to my dad.

My dad stopped emptying the dishwasher and gave me a huge hug. Meanwhile, I just kept on ranting, "I mean, I know I don't sing as well as her, but she's like this total Barbie clone. I hope she gets voted off in the first round!"

My dad didn't say anything. He's good about not trying to solve unsolvable problems. He wrinkled his forehead and squinted as if he were going to say something but never did. That just made me more upset, so I stomped back to my room and slammed the door.

Later on, I found this sticky note on my mirror. I could tell by the writing that it was from my dad. It was a Bible verse about that big green monster called jealousy.

Could Izzy Baxter be envious? Nah.

My Heart

If you harbor bitter envy and selfish ambition in your hearts, do not boast about it or deny the truth. Such "wisdom" does not come down from heaven but is earthly, unspiritual, of the devil. (James 3:14–15)

I admit, I am completely, insanely JEALOUS! Emily Elektra got what I wanted. She's gonna be traveling the world like some megastar while I get to stay home and do nothing pop starish at all.

I know, I know, this jealousy stuff is going to make my heartache worse. Envy is not a God thing, and I need to get rid of it. God wants us to live a life of love, and love is not jealous.

Good Night, God

Sorry for being so hard on Emily, God. I want what she has, and that makes me jealous. Lord, help me be glad for her instead. Help me know that You have great plans for me too. That way, this envy will fade away forever. Amen.

That's my prayer. What's yours?

L8R

---

2 COMMENTS:

James Baxter said . . .
I'm impressed.
Posted Thursday, 9:43 p.m.

Izzy said . . .
Sorry for being such a pain, Dad.
Posted Thursday, 9:57 p.m.

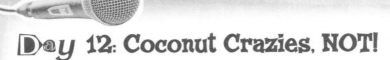

D@y 12: Coconut Crazies, NOT!

Mood Meter: Volcano Red

It's 10:30 at night and I am SO not tired. Ever since I was tragically rejected by *International Pop Star Challenge*, I've been too sad to catch any zzz's. Now, you need to know that when I'm bummed out and don't sleep well, I get over-the-top grumpy!!!

So this morning I got up to see that my brother had left the milk out on the counter all night. In Southern California, you never leave the milk out all night. GROSS! One sniff of the sour milk told me that I wouldn't be enjoying my daily bowl of Coconut Crazies. I mean, how rude to leave the milk out all night when your heartbroken sister needs breakfast!

Without thinking, I stomped into his room to give him a piece of my mind. I held the milk up high for him to see and then did something reeeeally bad. I *placed*—okay, I *threw* the carton on his bed. I saw the whole scene in slow motion. The carton landed, took a couple of bounces, and began pouring out all over his math project.

Now, you have to realize that Anders is a straight-A student. Sure, his penmanship stinks, but he spends hours on his math pages, even when he's on vacation! They look like works of art. I felt like I had spilled milk on the *Mona Lisa*.

You should have seen the look on his face when the curdled milk started running down his perfectly drawn bar graphs. Let's just say, he was more furious than furious, and I was in more trouble than trouble. I slowly backed out of his room, then ran like a mongoose down the hall.

I hid under my covers and hoped the whole incident would just go away, but it wouldn't. I knew I shouldn't have done that, but I was too embarrassed to go back and apologize. I avoided him all day, and that gave me time to rationalize the whole thing. "If he hadn't left the milk out, this whole sorry ordeal wouldn't have happened in the first place!"

About an hour ago, I read this verse about not letting the sun go down while you are still angry, and I knew I couldn't go to sleep without apologizing. I nervously walked to his room, took a deep breath, and stepped in. He was playing his Xbox. I gently sat on his bed and gave him a hug. Sobbing like a baby, I blurted out, "I'm so sorry!"

Surprisingly, he didn't even yell at me for messing up his game. He awkwardly hugged me back and said something like, "Sorry for the milk." Then he just turned around and went back to playing *Earth Crisis Two*.

You know, I'm starting to think that my brother is a pretty cool dude, even if he does leave the milk out sometimes.

My Heart

"In your anger, do not sin." Do not let the sun go down while you are still angry. (Ephesians 4:26)

Everyone gets angry sometimes. I mean, people can be over-the-top frustrating sometimes. The hard part is not to sin when we're angry. You know, like trash-talking the person who hurt us to every other human in sight, or throwing milk on someone's math project.

The Bible says not to let the sun go down while you're still angry. So talk it out, ask for forgiveness if you need to, and let go. Holding on to anger is like holding on to fire, OUCH!

Good Night, God

Lord, my brother is awesome! Thanks for reminding me to work things out with Anders before bed tonight. Amen.

That's my prayer. What's yours?

L8R

---

2 COMMENTS:

Pastor Ryan said . . .
Preach it, Iz! By the way, you're still leading worship for group Monday night, right?
Posted Friday, 10:52 p.m.

Izzy said . . .
Not this week. I think I'm through with music. Sorry.
Posted Friday, 11:04 p.m.

Day 13: Sandcastles

Mood Meter: Figuring Things Out

When I was like six, I built this huge sandcastle by the Santa Monica pier. I worked all day on that thing. It started out small, but then my mom, dad, and brother started helping out. After about an hour, that thing was huge! It had seven towers, and this cool balcony on the front. I ran up to my beach bag to get my princess figures so that I could put them in the castle, but then tragedy struck. A wave about the size of Mount Everest completely wiped my dream castle away. I was so upset; my parents couldn't even cheer me up with ice cream.

I feel the same way today, MAD! I had all these big plans, hopes of becoming this famous singer, hopes of traveling the world, and now I have nothing! I'm stuck with my ordinary life, in my ordinary room, with my ordinary brother hogging the bathroom again. I wish I had never gone to that audition in the first place!

Usually I try to calm down before praying. But tonight I was too upset to even do that. I ended up being totally and completely honest with God. I told Him how disappointed I was. I told Him how confused I was. I even told Him I was angry.

I wasn't disrespectful or anything, just honest. It felt good. I mean, God already knows what I'm feeling anyway, so I might as pray it.

Oh yeah, I got over the whole castle thing lightning quick. I spent the rest of the afternoon hopping waves with my mom and forgot all about it. I guess I'll get over this whole *International Pop Star Challenge* thing one day also, when I'm about EIGHTY!

My Heart

"Come now, let us reason together," says the LORD. *(Isaiah 1:18)*

Our prayers don't have to be all holy and perfectly worked out. It's totally okay to reason with God. That means we can fully share what's on our minds. If we're mad, we can be mad. If we're sad, we can be sad. God wants to hear our side of the story, emotions and all.

Good Night, God

I'm a little bit confused, sad, and really mad tonight, Lord. Help me be honest with You. Help me get over all these messy feelings. Amen.

That's my prayer. What's yours?

L8R

---

3 COMMENTS:

Anders said . . .
When Mom died, I was so mad I didn't talk to God for, like, three weeks.
Posted Saturday, 9:07 p.m.

Pastor Ryan said . . .
And God had His arms around you anyway, Anders.
Posted Saturday, 9:33 p.m.

Anders said . . .
Yeah, I know. We're good now. ☺
Posted Saturday, 9:52 p.m.

D@y 14: Ms. Adelina

Mood Meter: Silently Sad

You'll be amazed to hear that I'm actually blogging during sunshine hours today. I didn't feel like hanging around church talking to my friends like I usually do, so I just walked home. I didn't want everyone asking me about the show and stuff, too painful.

My dad usually drives to church, but I love walking. The fifteen-minute walk takes you past some pretty historic parts of Hollywood, places like the Roosevelt Hotel, where the first Academy Awards were held. When I walk, I imagine what it was like back in the 1940s when Hollywood was booming.

My apartment building is pretty historic itself. Way back when, a lot of up-and-coming actors and actresses used to live here. This cowboy star called Tex Samuels lived in the apartment across the hall, and Beth Mayfield once slept in the third-floor hallway when she locked herself out of her place.

The building is pretty old now, but I love it. I love the chipped paint and funky brickwork. I just love everything about it, especially the people. Since the building is in Hollywood, a lot of artist-type people move in here. It's fun having all that creativity around.

The best thing about my building is the nightly concert by Ms. Adelina. Ms. Adelina Gabriella Farinelli is the elegant seventy-eight-year-old lady who lives directly below me. She's absolutely gorgeous. I heard she used to be an opera singer in her homeland, Argentina.

Every night at exactly 7:30 p.m., she comes out onto her balcony and sings while she tends to her garden. It's always the same song, "Violeta." It's in Spanish, so I have absolutely no idea what the words mean, but it's outrageously beautiful. When she sings, I forget about all my worries and just lose myself in the sad, sweet melody.

I'm not the only Ms. Adelina fan in the building. Every time she's out there, you can see other tenants on their balconies dreaming along with the aria.

My whole life flipped upside down when my mom died. Everything, I mean absolutely EVERYTHING, changed. But with all those changes, I knew that one thing would always be the same. At 7:30 each night, a beautiful Argentine woman would step out onto the balcony of apartment 14D and paint the night with her song. For some reason, that gave me peace.

Anyway, gotta go. Dad and Anders just came home.

My Heart

Jesus Christ is the same yesterday and today and forever.
(Hebrews 13:8)

I can always count on Ms. Adelina's singing. If I'm sick, she sings. If I have a bad school day, she sings. Every night it's exactly the same. That reminds me of God's love. It never changes. If I fail a test, God loves me. If someone hurts my feelings, He loves me. If I never, ever become a pop star, He still loves me. His love never changes.

Good Night, God

In all this crazy disappointment, help me remember that Your love always stays the same. Amen.
That's my prayer. What's yours?
L8R

---

3 COMMENTS:

Pastor Ryan said . . .
I was wondering where you ran off to after church. I was going to beg you to lead worship tomorrow night. Come on, Iz, pleeeeeeeze!!
Posted Sunday, 3:27 p.m.

Izzy said . . .
Not yet. Maybe in a couple of weeks or something.
Posted Sunday, 4:22 p.m.

Pastor Ryan said . . .
All right, I guess the group can survive my singing for one night. Just know that Steph and I are praying for you.
Posted Sunday, 8:43 p.m.

Day 15: Friends

Mood Meter: What's This? A Smile?

I think God was trying to get through to me today. Check this out.

While I was brushing my teeth this morning, my cell beeped. It was a text from Maddie: "R U OK?"

I immediately felt guilty because I hadn't called, texted, or even bird mailed her since the *Pop Star Challenge* tragedy. I rinsed out my mouth and put down the phone. *I'll text her later*, I thought.

Then, I walked into the kitchen and saw Maddie sitting with my dad. Before I could even say hi, Maddie got up and gave me this huge hug. "Those producers made a massive mistake, Iz," she said as she patted my back. "I'm never watching that show again!"

I was about to start bawling, but before I could she grabbed my hand and started pulling me to the door. "I know just the thing to cheer you up!" she said as she whisked me toward LuLu's.

We sat there for at least two hours. She listened as I spilled my soul over a chocolate chip muffin. Ezequiel, the manager, must have seen me crying because he didn't charge us anything and let us sit for as long as we wanted. Maddie basically told me I needed to get on with my life, and not let my disappointment take over. At first I didn't want to listen, but deep down I knew she was right.

I spent the day thinking about what she said. In all my pain, I had been pretty self-centered. That *definitely* needed to change.

I picked up my guitar, headed to the fire escape, and started playing. Just feeling the strings moving under my fingers made me feel better. I actually finished "Wait," the song I had started awhile back. When I was done, I looked at the clock and realized that group had started. If I hurried, I could get there in time for worship. I flung my guitar over my shoulder and ran to church, BAREFOOT!

I burst through the door just as Pastor Ryan was finishing a worship song. He smiled and called me up to the stage. When I took over, I could tell he was relieved.

At the end of my set, I decided to play "Wait." I set the lyrics in front of me and began to sing. Everything was going fine until I got to the bridge:

Hold me gently, sing Your lullaby to me.
Lift me higher, high enough so I can see
'Cause all life's noise is drowning out Your plans for me.
Please, can You help me wait?

The leaky faucet of tears started. At first it was just a trickle, but then I couldn't help it. I started bawling. I couldn't even finish the song. Before I could run off the stage in embarrassment, I felt a warm hand on my shoulder and then another. Before long, the entire youth group was up onstage praying for me.

As I listened to their prayers, I felt like God was giving me a huge hug. Even though nothing on the pop star front had changed, I knew, then and there, that everything was going to be okay.

My Heart

When Moses' hands grew tired, they took a stone and put it under him and he sat on it. Aaron and Hur held his hands up—one on one side, one on the other—so that his hands remained steady till sunset. (Exodus 17:12)

This verse comes from a really cool story in the Bible. I heard it at group a few weeks ago. The Israelites were fighting the Amalekites. As long as Moses kept his arms raised, the Israelites were winning. Of course his arms were, like, exhausted after a while. So his friends Aaron and Hur each grabbed an arm and held them up for him. Moses couldn't do it alone, but with his friends he could.

Sometimes we think we can get through life's disappointments on our own, but we can't. We need our family and friends to lift our arms up, just like Aaron and Hur did for Moses.

Good Night, God

Thanks, God, for friends. Even though it still hurts, I don't feel alone, and that feels awesome! Amen.
That's my prayer. What's yours?
L8R

2 COMMENTS:

Sabine said . . .
Awesome song, Iz, tears and all!
Posted Monday, 10:39 p.m.

Izzy said . . .
The tears were for dramatic effect, you know (ha ha). Thanks for the
    prayer!! Hopefully we can hang this week.
Posted Monday, 10:57 p.m.

D@y 16: Operation Love

Mood Meter: Yes, It Is a Smile!

My dad let me sleep in today because we were up late talking last night. Well, I was doing all the talking. He just kind of listened.

After I finished blogging on the fire escape, I heard this noise behind me. I was shocked to see my dad crawl through the window and sit beside me. Now you may be thinking, *What's the big deal about that?* Well, it is a big deal. My dad never comes out onto the fire escape with me. My mom was the one who did that kind of stuff. She and I would sit out there all the time and just quietly think together, side by side. But my dad, we've never really hung out together that much, especially lately. Ever since Mom died, he's been kind of in his own world.

Anyway, I told my dad EVERYTHING last night, about how group went, and about how I'm so ready to move on from all the pain and disappointment. At one point I even shouted, "I, Izzy Baxter, am ready to move on!"

Then Mr. McGuire yelled, "I, Eugene McGuire, am ready for Izzy Baxter to go to bed!!"

My dad and I started cracking up, and we laughed for like ten minutes straight. When it was time for bed, I felt, I don't know, like happy again!

When I woke up today, the happiness was still there. Even though it's summer vacation, I wished my dad hadn't let me sleep so long. I had been kind of self-centered for the last couple weeks or so, and there was a lot of catching up to do. I hopped out of bed and got to work on Operation Love.

First off, I sent Maddie a good morning text: "Shiny morning!" I hadn't sent her a text in like a week, so I was sure she would appreciate that.

Next, I made some lemonade with tons of ice for my dad and took it to his office. He smiled a bright rainbow smile when I walked in. I was off to a good start.

After that, I emptied the dishwasher, my brother's chore for the week. Boy, is he going to be surprised when he gets home from the beach bonfire tonight.

Finally, I skipped downstairs for my final deed of the day. Awhile back, Ms. Adelina mentioned to my dad that someone had given her a laptop so she could e-mail her brother in Argentina. She had no idea how to create an account, though. So I, super teen blogging machine, set up her e-mail for her. I even taught her how to get to my blog. Pretty cool, huh?

I was so busy with Operation Love that I didn't even think about *Pop Star* until noon. A new record! You know, I think I could get used to this giving stuff.

Oh yeah, I almost forgot. The best thing about today was that about an hour ago, my dad came out onto the fire escape, AGAIN. This time he was carrying two cups of hot chocolate, just like my mom used to do. I guess I'm not the only one ready to move on.

My Heart
Do nothing out of selfish ambition or vain conceit, but in humility consider others better than yourselves. Each of you should look not only to your own interests, but also to the interests of others. (Philippians 2:3–4)

You know, in all my disappointment, I totally started focusing on myself. It was like everyone around me didn't exist. But today, when I was helping people out, I realized something. I was made to love. I think we were *all* made to love. It's like when we love others, we forget about our own problems, and things start to feel right again. Long live love!

Good Night, God
Hey, God, thanks for the wonderful distraction of love. Amen.
That's my prayer. What's yours?
L8R

---

2 COMMENTS:

Ms. Adelina said . . .
I just send my first e-mail to my brother Marcelo in Argentina. Thank you for you help. I feel like an angel come and visit me today.
Posted Tuesday, 10:09 p.m.

Izzy said . . .
You are totally welcome, Ms. Adelina. I'm just excited you can read my blog now!!!
Posted Tuesday, 10:54 p.m.

D@y 17: No Way!

Mood Meter: Speechless

Okay, you better sit down for this blog. It's pretty over the top. Let me take a couple of deep breaths first. . . . Now I think I'm ready.

I'M GOING TO BE ON *INTERNATIONAL POP STAR CHALLENGE*! It's true. It's true. It's true! It's totally, unbelievably unbelievable! About an hour ago, my dad got a call from the producer of the show. Of course, I hit the speakerphone button, to make sure I heard every word. Anyway, he said that Emily Elektra wouldn't sign her *Pop Star Challenge* contract. Apparently, her agent was upset about some of the rules of the show or something. She's decided to sign a contract with Worldbeat Records instead.

Unbelievable, I know. So the producer asked my dad if I wanted to take her place on the show. Well, it took all of about two milliseconds to decide. I yelled into the phone speaker, "YES!!!"

After my dad hung up, I hugged my brother and started crying, happy tears, of course. Then we cranked up some music and danced around the kitchen until we couldn't dance anymore. We used to do that a lot when someone had good news, but we kind of gave up on that tradition after Mom died. It was really cool to dance again.

"Let's go down to LuLu's to celebrate!" my dad yelled as he grabbed his wallet.

"Just give me a few minutes," I screamed as I ran down the hall toward my room. "There's someone I need to talk to first!"

You see, my mom used to always say, "Cry with God when you're sad, and celebrate with Him when you're happy." Well, I had definitely done a lot of crying with God over the last couple of years, so I wasn't about to celebrate without Him.

With a warm breeze blowing in my face, I climbed out onto my usual spot, lifted my hands to heaven, and got the party started. "God, You've been listening to all my prayers!" I squealed, not caring who heard me. "Because of You, my dreams are truly coming true. Because of You, I get to sing! Thank You!"

My Heart

Many, O Lᴏʀᴅ my God, are the wonders you have done. The things you planned for us no one can recount to you; were I to speak and tell of them, they would be too many to declare. (Psalm 40:5)

Don't just talk to God when you need something from Him. Remember to pray when you are happy too. Sing, dance, and praise Him for all the cool things He's done.

Good Night, God

Lord, I praise You for good news phone calls and kitchen dances. I praise You for all the sweet surprises You pull from out of the blue. Thanks! Amen.

That's my prayer. What's yours?

Now it's double berry smoothie time with Maddie and the fam! Gotta go!

L8R

---

3 COMMENTS:

Pastor Ryan said . . .
Yay, Izzy!! God is good!
Posted Wednesday, 7:22 p.m.

Sabine said . . .
Awesome! Can I have your autograph?
Posted Wednesday, 8:07 p.m.

Stephanie said . . .
Now the whole world gets to hear what we hear each week!
Posted Wednesday, 8:15 p.m.

D@y 18: Quest Studios

Mood Meter: Intimidated

"Rise and shine, Iz," my brother yelled as he pulled open the shades. "Time for *Pop Star* madness!" Usually I would cover my head with my pillow and fall back asleep, but not today. In fact, I had been awake with excitement for most of the night. Today was the day that my *International Pop Star Challenge* adventure would begin.

Yesterday, while we were celebrating at LuLu's, someone from *Pop Star* called my dad and told him I had to be at Quest Studios by 6:30 in the morning for a preproduction meeting. So at—get this— *five in the morning*, I got up and got ready to go. Not bad for a girl who spends her summer days sleeping till eleven.

I started feeling reeeeeally nervous as we got closer and closer to the studio. By the time we drove through the gates, I felt like I was going to throw up.

When I walked into the production offices, Renee Shappelle, the show's publicist, greeted me by name in the lobby. As she led me down a long hallway, she cheerfully explained that the other nineteen contestants had flown in the night before and were now waiting in the conference room.

Okay, I need to explain something: this conference room was HUGE. It wasn't just a room with a table running down the middle. It was more like an auditorium, with a stage and everything. There must have been like eighty people in there. Renee led me to a seat in the front row. My dad quietly found a seat in the back.

The show's judges, Aiko Mae, Marshall Phillips, and Giuseppe Rossi, sat behind a table on the stage along with some other people I didn't recognize.

The show's director, Werner Ballack, spoke first. He greeted us and spent like two hours going over the rules of the show, our schedules, and even the travel arrangements. I turned around and saw my dad taking total notes, so that was good.

After that, each of the contestants had to come onstage and introduce themselves. They called my name first since I was the only American contestant, and I just about totally freaked out. I reminded myself of Pop Star Plan Rule #11—"When you're screaming scared on the inside, smile sweetly on the outside"—and walked confidently up to the stage.

It was pretty easy, actually. They asked me about my past experience in the entertainment industry, NONE, and some basic stuff about my family. They finished the interview by showing a tape of my audition. It was weird seeing my face staring down at the audience from the huge screen they had up front.

Since I was done first, I should have been able to relax, but I couldn't. As I watched each singer speak, I became more and more intimidated. There was this pink-haired girl from Japan named Atsumi who could hit notes I didn't even know existed. Another singer, twenty-year-old Colleen Leary, had been in countless London musicals. Then there was this really trendy sixteen-year-old guy named Etienne Rousseau who was already a star in France.

As if I weren't intimidated enough, Giuseppe Rossi closed off the meeting by saying, "People, this is not the playground anymore. This is big time. If you cannot handle the pressure, you should go home now."

As I headed toward the car with my dad, it dawned on me: I'm in completely over my head!

My Heart

I can do everything through him who gives me strength.
(Philippians 4:13)

My dad told me this verse in the car today, and it made me think. I can't handle this whole *Pop Star Challenge* thing on my own. I can't, but God *can*. It was a miracle that I even made the show. If God placed me here, He'll give me the strength to handle it.

Do you ever feel overwhelmed by things? Do you have a problem that you feel like you can't handle? Just remember, God will get you through.

Good Night, God

Lord, I'm in over my head, but You're not. Help me remember that. Amen.

That's my prayer. What's yours?

L8R

---

2 COMMENTS:

Ms. Adelina said . . .

When I sing at La Scala, my hands shake like the wings of a hummingbird, but when I begin to sing, then my hands are still once more. I tell you more when you come for tea tomorrow. Okay?

Posted Thursday, 8:43 p.m.

Maddie said . . .

Take a deep breath, Iz. It's gonna all work out.

Posted Thursday, 9:15 p.m.

Day 19: Time for Team

Mood Meter: Nervously Overjoyed

Okay, I mentioned yesterday that there were about eighty people at the meeting. Who were these people, you ask?

Well, let me explain. Every singer there, except for me and maybe like two others, had a group of people with them. There were parents, agents, and even personal stylists! Add that to all the *Pop Star* staff, and you've got one crowded room.

So today I've been on a mission, a team-building mission. Pop Star Plan Rule #21 says, "Do what you have to do, and do it well." So if I have to have a team in order to be excellent, I'll get one.

I set out to find the perfect Izzy crew. I had to be a little creative, since my family doesn't have a money tree growing in our rooftop garden.

I started with the obvious, Maddie. She absolutely lives and breathes fashion. She even sews her own outfits sometimes, really funky and cool. I know the show will want me to use their own stylist, but I still want Maddie to help somehow. I mean, she knows what looks good, and more important, she knows me. I asked her if she wanted to maybe dream up some outfits for me to wear on the show. She screamed, "Yes!" so loud that her mom came in to see what was wrong.

Next, I needed a vocal coach, someone who really knew what they were doing. Suddenly it came to me—Ms. Adelina! I jogged down to her apartment and rang the doorbell. When she saw my face, she gave me a kiss on each cheek and welcomed me in. She brought out some tea, and I told her all about the *Pop Star* meeting and about how a lot of the singers had vocal coaches. When I asked her if she wanted to be my coach, she hesitated.

"I not so sure, Preciosa," she answered calmly.

I explained how she wouldn't have to travel with me or anything. "You can just watch my performances on TV and post tips on my blog," I begged.

"I tell you another day." She smiled as she picked up our empty teacups.

I helped Ms. Adelina wash the dishes and headed home for my last appointment. I needed a manager, someone who knew the music scene inside and out, someone who was smart. The perfect candidate lived in the bedroom across from me, Anders.

Now, you need to know something about my brother: he is mellow with a capital *M*. When I asked him to be my manager, he just said, "Cool," and that was that. I had my manager.

The cool thing about having Anders on board is that he'll be traveling with me. Two people can travel with us, and so I'm taking my family, of course.

Photo shoot and packing tomorrow, off to Tokyo on Sunday. I can't wait!

My Heart

Two are better than one, because they have a good return for their work. If one falls down, his friend can help him up. But pity the man who falls and has no one to help him up! (Ecclesiastes 4:9–10)

I feel really good about the people I've surrounded myself with. They love me. They love God, and I can trust them.

You don't have to be a pop star to have a team like that. Everyone needs a solid crew around to give them advice and help them up when they fall down. I guess we were MADE TO BE TOGETHER. (Hey, that would be a great song title!)

Good Night, God

Lord, give all of us wisdom as we head off into the wild unknown, together. Amen.

That's my prayer. What's yours?

By the way guys, thanks for listening to my highs and heartaches over the last couple of weeks. You've all been on my team from the start. L8R

---

2 COMMENTS:

Ms. Adelina said . . .
Okay, I do it. But if I coach, you must listen.
Posted Friday, 8:02 p.m.

Izzy said . . .
Yay! I won't let you down, Ms. Adelina.
Posted Friday, 10:17 p.m.

Pastor Ryan said . . .
Hey, if you ever need a backup singer, I'm available.
Posted Friday, 10:32 p.m.

Day 20: Photo Shoot

Mood Meter: Mixed

Today was totally, insanely crazy. I got up early, AGAIN, to go down to Quest Studios for my very first ever promo shoot. They wanted to take video footage and pictures of us for the opening of the show.

So anyway, after breakfast in the commissary (anything you want, for free!), we headed over to this makeup trailer. Christine, one of the show's three makeup artists, spent an entire hour working on my hair and face. She put on this cool sparkly eye shadow, and used some magical mascara that made my eyelashes look huge. Everything she used had red, white, or blue tones, since I was going to wear those colors during the shoot. My hair looked kind of messy, but I totally loooooved it.

After a couple of final hair spray blasts, Renee came in and said they were ready for me. I headed over to studio 42, where they had this entirely white room. There were cameras all over the place, and a zillion lights.

They had me stand on this circle on the floor, and the modeling madness began. They took like a thousand pictures and shot video footage. At one point, they blasted this fan toward me, and my hair was blowing all over, pretty cool. I'm kind of embarrassed to say this, but I've been practicing supermodel moves in front of the mirror for like ten years now, so the whole posing thing came kind of easy.

I'm in my room right now, taking a break from packing. My flight leaves tomorrow morning at nine. The studio is sending a limo to pick us up. Awesome!

Anyway, I have all the stuff I'm packing spread out on the bed. Besides clothes, I'm taking Coco the monkey, my MP3 player, four packs of sour ropes (because I doubt they have those in Japan), and definitely my brand-new Bible. My dad bought it for me this week. It's travel size and it fits in my pocket, totally tiny!

I'm going to head down to Ms. Adelina's for a quick visit and then to LuLu's. Since I'm going to be gone for a looooong time, my friends are meeting me there to say good-bye . . . sniff, sniff.

This is going to be one crazy cool summer.

My Heart

Your word is a lamp to my feet and a light for my path.
(Psalm 119:105)

My dad wrote this verse in the inside cover of my new Bible, so I see it each night when I read. It reminds me that the Bible is not just some book of nice stories. It's like a light guiding us through life. It's God's Word.

Good Night, God

Lord, help the Bible come alive to me. Help me understand it, and let it be a light shining on the foggy roads in front of me. Amen. That's my prayer. What's yours?
L8R

---

3 COMMENTS:

Stephanie said . . .
You will be totally missed around here. Ryan and I have put you on our prayer list, so every night you can count on us praying for you.
Posted Saturday, 10:37 p.m.

Maddie said . . .
WAAAAAAAH! Three months is too long. What am I going to do without my best bud?
Posted Saturday, 10:56 p.m.

Izzy said . . .
I'll only be gone three months if I make it to the finals. I doubt that will ever happen. But even a week seems like forever. ☹
Posted Saturday, 11:32 p.m.

PART 2

Harajuku Highlife

I want to sing, sing, sing . . .
I just want to lift my hands,
And give you everything I am.

"SING"—IZZY BAXTER

Day 21: Tokyo

Mood Meter: Definitely Dazed

After eleven insanely long hours in the air, I've finally found a bed to crash on. That's about all I know. I'm in a total jet-lagged daze. According to my Monkey Mon watch, it's 10:15 p.m. on Sunday, in Los Angeles. The clock in my Tokyo hotel room, though, says it's 2:15 in the afternoon ON MONDAY! I'm like crazy confused. It'll take a while to get used to this whole time change business.

We're staying in the Ginza district of Tokyo. Renee told me on the plane that it's an awesome place to shop—if you have a lot of cash, that is. I'm on the 43rd floor of this huge skyscraper hotel. I'm sitting on my windowsill, and down below I can see zillions of people walking around like ants. There are neon lights and huge billboards *everywhere*. Of course they're all in Japanese, so I don't understand a thing.

This whole day has been kind of confusing, actually, and I feel a bit of homesickness coming on, already! I'm such a wimp.

Anyway, that's the FYI on me. Gotta go crash now.

L8R

---

2 COMMENTS:

Ms. Adelina said . . .
"If I rise on the wings of the dawn, if I settle on the far side of the sea, even there your hand will guide me, your right hand will hold me fast"
(Psalm 139:9–10).
Preciosa, no matter where you going, He come with you.
Posted Monday, 10:35 a.m.

Stephanie said . . .

Father in heaven, help Izzy realize that even though You've sent her clear
across the Pacific Ocean and everything seems different, You won't
abandon her. Amen.

Posted Monday, 11:43 a.m.

Day 22: Rules, Rules, Rules

Mood Meter: Dancing (Literally)

Sorry about yesterday's blog. I was just tired. I'm still not over jet lag, but I'm starting to feel excited again. This morning we had breakfast at the hotel and drove off to Tama Studios, which is about thirty minutes outside of Tokyo. I can't get over the fact that I'm actually in Japan!

We had an ages-long meeting there, where they introduced us to the Japanese film crew and went over the rules of the show, as if we didn't already know. In case you're one of the two people left on Earth who hasn't seen *Pop Star Challenge* yet, here's how the show works.

There are twenty of us in Japan. In a couple of days, we'll tape our first show: Challenge Night. During that show, the judges will give us our first challenge. The challenges are always a surprise, but they usually have to do with singing, like writing a song or shooting a video or something. Contestants are then given like a week to plan out or rehearse for whatever the challenge is. While we're planning—this part completely freaks me out—a camera crew will be following us around, for up to five hours a day! They'll be watching us rehearse, talk on the phone, eat, EVERYTHING! They'll use this footage on the Update show, where the TV audience sees how we're doing so far. I'll have to watch everything I say and do, because the viewers are the ones who vote you through to the next round.

Then comes Performance Night. That's the BIG show where we perform and the three judges rate us. What they say is really important, because TV viewers listen to their opinions, especially Giuseppe. He scares me. I've seen him rip contestants apart until they were in tears. On the other hand, if he says you did well, you can pretty much pack your bags for the next round. After the show, *Pop Star Challenge* viewers have exactly twenty-four hours to text in votes for their favorite singers.

Finally, there's the results show, or Vote Night. That's where they tell us the results of the voting. The top ten singers move on to the next round in Paris, and the rest go home. I'M SHAKING ALREADY!

The next round is exactly the same, with five singers moving on to Buenos Aires, Argentina. Finally, the top two singers will head to New York for the finals.

Anyway, that's how it all works. I better wrap this up; I need to wake up before the camera crew gets to my hotel room. There is NO WAY that they are going to catch my nightmarish morning hair on film. Yikes!

My Heart

"Can anyone hide in secret places so that I cannot see him?" declares the LORD. *"Do not I fill heaven and earth?"* declares the LORD. *(Jeremiah 23:24)*

Okay, I'm pretty freaked out about having a camera crew follow me around. They'll be watching everything I do for, like, five hours a day. I mean, come on, they'll probably be taping me eating my Coconut Crazies in the morning!

I thought of something today. God is everywhere too. Like the camera crew, He hears everything we say and watches every move we make. So whether the cameras are on or off, we need to live our lives like God is watching.

Good Night, God

Lord, help me always be aware of Your eyes on me. That'll help me stay on track. Amen.

That's my prayer. What's yours?

L8R

---

2 COMMENTS:

Maddie said . . .
I wish I could see you too! Your bedroom looks so dark and empty, sniff, sniff. I'll just have to wait for Challenge Night on Friday.
Posted Tuesday, 5:38 p.m.

Ms. Adelina said . . .
Preciosa, make sure you take care of that voice. Lots of water and no desserts on the day of you sing!!
Posted Tuesday, 7:02 p.m.

Day 23: Who Are You?

Mood Meter: Like a Beach Ball, PUMPED!

"Good morning, good morning!" said the smiling Japanese camera duo as they walked into the hotel restaurant this morning. One had a medium-sized camera on his shoulder, and the other, a girl, held a fuzzy mike on this small pole thing. Luckily, I had gotten up early enough to do my hair and makeup. (Whew!) Other than tell me their names, Kenji and Miya, they pretty much said nothing. AWKWARD!

I was supposed to act "normal," but that was pretty much impossible. I mean, being followed around by a camera crew on the streets of Tokyo isn't really part of my usual daily routine.

Like a big happy family, we hopped into the limo and headed to Tama Studios for our first rehearsal. I tried to make small talk with my brother on the way, but with the cameras in his face, he froze like an ice cube. He wouldn't say a word! He just sat there nervously smiling and nodding like a bobblehead.

I told him how beautiful I thought Tokyo was. He nodded. I told him how friendly I thought the people were. He nodded. He even nodded when I asked him what his favorite Japanese cartoon was! Tell me, how does nodding "yes" even answer that question?

I was getting frustrated with him, but, of course, I couldn't show it. As long as that little red light on the camera kept blinking, I was all smiles.

I was relieved to find Christine, the stylist, waiting for me in the parking lot. Finally, someone who would actually talk to me!

Christine didn't seem fazed at all by the cameras. She cheerfully led me to the wardrobe department and told me to have a seat. There, among rows and rows of awesome-looking outfits, we talked fashion. Christine knew everything there was to know about what was "in" and what was not.

"Who are you?" she asked as she tossed around strands of my long hair.

I wasn't sure how to answer and just kind of sat there.

"How do you want the world to see you?" she went on. "Are you punk, indie, a rocker, maybe a songwriter hippie type?"

"To be honest, I don't really know," I stuttered as the camera rolled on. "I mean, sure, I like certain styles, but that's not who I really am."

Christine was cool about my answer and just started grabbing outfits off the racks. I told her which ones I liked and which ones I didn't. Every once in a while, she would write something down on a yellow notepad. After about an hour, she seemed satisfied and sent me to this huge sound stage where the rest of the contestants were waiting.

Rehearsals were crazy fun. We learned where to stand during Friday's taping and got the music for our first song, a full group number. The show is going to open with it, pretty cool. Everyone here is such an over-the-top singer, so it's awesome hearing all our voices together!

The cameras stopped following me around at about four—WHAT A RELIEF—and we all headed back to our hotel for dinner.

As I walked exhaustedly into the lobby, I saw Christine again. "Remember, you have homework tonight," she said as she stepped into an elevator. "Who are you?"

People, heeeelp! WHO AM I?

My Heart

For you created my inmost being; you knit me together in my mother's womb. I praise you because I am fearfully and wonderfully made; your works are wonderful, I know that full well. (Psalm 139:13–14)

"Who are you?" Come on! That's a tough question to answer. I don't know who I am, at least not yet. The cool thing, though, is that God does. He's the One who knows who we *really* are. He made us and had plans for us before we were even born.

So if you're wondering who you are, ask God. He can fill you in on the details.

Good Night, God

Lord, who am I? I really want to know. Amen.
That's my prayer. What's yours?
L8R

Maddie said . . .
I'm on it, boss. We'll figure it out.
Posted Wednesday, 5:30 p.m.

Ms. Adelina said . . .
You're a singer. You were born to sing.
Posted Wednesday, 6:32 p.m.

James Baxter said . . .
You're a girl who wears her heart on her sleeve, just like her mother. And
you'll always be my sweetest little Iz.
Posted Wednesday, 7:32 p.m.

Pastor Ryan said . . .
You were made to worship, definitely.
Posted Wednesday, 8:07 p.m.

Stephanie said . . .
You are an awesome young woman of God, and my dear friend.
Posted Wednesday, 8:54 p.m.

D@y 24: Monkey Madness

Mood Meter: Curious Like Maddie's Cat

Konnichiwa!

That means "hi," in case you're wondering. I've been trying to learn some Japanese using this dictionary the studio gave us. I've learned tons already.

Let's see, um, *arigato* means "thank you," and *sumimasen* means "excuse me." I use that one all the time, since I'm constantly bumping into people in this mega crowded city. The one sentence I use the most, though, is *Nihongo ga wakarimasen*, which means "I don't speak Japanese!"

I actually got to use some Japanese today because after rehearsals in the morning, we got to go on a field trip. They took us all to Mt. Takao, which is about an hour away from downtown Tokyo. It's the first time any of us, besides Atsumi, had been outside of the city, so we were all oohing and aahing and snapping away with our cell phone cameras.

Of course Kenji and Miya were there too, with their ever-present cameras, but I didn't really mind. I'm kind of getting used to having them around. It was crazy cool. We took this cable car to the top of the mountain and got to see some Japanese snow monkeys. AWESOME!

I hung out with Colleen for most of the day. She's kind of into the whole "goth" thing, you know, black makeup and clothes, listens to Zombie Rush all the time. I'm not really into that scene, but, hey, she's from England, so I was just glad I could actually understand what she was saying.

Oh yeah, Etienne hung out with us too. You would never guess that he's a big pop star in France, totally humble guy. He actually speaks English pretty well. He told me his name is French for Stephen. Doesn't the name Etienne sound so cool, compared to our boring old American names?

The other contestants are totally nice also. They all speak some English, because you have to if you want to be on the show, but a lot of them don't speak it very well. One long-haired guy, Miklos—I don't know where he's from—kept on coming up to me and saying, "America, ROCK AND ROLL!" I think those are some of the only English words he knows. We both laugh when he says it, but by, like, the tenth time, I started thinking, *Get over it already, dude!*

At the end of the day, all twenty of us just sat on these rocks and watched the sun set over Tokyo. There we were, twenty kids from all over the world, speaking different languages, just hanging out together. It was amazingly amazing!

I am so going to have a mind-blowing time on this show.

My Heart

He said to them, "Go into all the world and preach the good news to all creation." (Mark 16:15)

As I sat on that mountain today, a knock-my-socks-off truth hit me. There are so many people on this earth! They're all so different and have unique histories, hopes, and dreams. The cool thing is that God loves all of them, every single one, no matter where they're from. Our job is to spread that good news to all the world.

Maybe that's why I'm here.

Good Night, God

Lord, help me spread Your good news wherever I go. Amen.
That's my prayer. What's yours?
Ja mata! (L8R in Japanese!)

---

2 COMMENTS:

Maddie said . . .
Have you figured out who you are yet? Just kidding! I am working on the perfect "YOU" outfit design right now. More news later!
Posted Thursday, 7:05 a.m.

Izzy said . . .
Cool! I can't wait to see it. Maybe you can e-mail it to me, and the *Pop Star* wardrobe people can check it out?
Posted Thursday, 7:11 a.m.

D@y 25: Challenge Night

Mood Meter: Adrenaline Rush!

"Twenty talented singers from twenty nations, twenty hearts full of pop star dreams. Coming to you live from Tokyo, Japan; it's season eight of *International Pop Star Challenge*!"

When Sean Moore, the show's host, gave his trademark opening tonight, I had to pinch myself. *Is this actually happening?* I thought as I waited backstage. I mean, little Izzy Baxter was about to step on stage and perform in front of millions of TV viewers around the world. It was just totally unreal.

Was I nervous? Not one bit! I was insanely excited. I've been dreaming of a moment like this for the last ten years. In fact, I've been *planning* for a moment like this for the last ten years. As we got our cue to go onstage, I intended to enjoy every second of the experience.

We opened the show with this disco song called "Dance the World Away." I know what you're thinking, kind of cheesy, but it sounded really good.

We all came onstage at different times in groups of four. I was with Etienne, Atsumi, and Colleen. We came in from behind these flags singing, "Listen to the music / spread your voice around the world!" We had this awesome harmony going on, and the Japanese crowd in the studio was on their feet dancing. I don't think I've ever had more fun in my entire life.

Then they showed our audition tapes and footage of our opening days in Japan. Luckily, Kenji and Miya hadn't filmed anything embarrassing. I'm sure Anders didn't appreciate the shots of his terrified, camera-shy face in the limo, though. The audience thought that was funny.

The only time I did get a little nervous was when challenge time came. This Japanese model came onstage carrying an envelope. There was this drum roll while Aiko Mae opened it. Then she read the challenge inside.

"As a pop star you will need to make choices, choices that will determine the course of your career. Make the wrong one, and your career may come to an end," she said. I could tell she already knew what the challenge was going to be, because she wasn't reading from the paper anymore.

"This week's challenge is all about choices," she continued. "You must choose the location of your first performance in Japan. The location of this eight-song concert is entirely up to you."

So there it is; my first challenge. I have twelve days to set up my first ever concert in a place where I don't even speak the language. YIKES!

My Heart

Whatever you do, work at it with all your heart, as working for the Lord, not for men. (Colossians 3:23)

Okay, I admit, I'm in way over my head. I don't know a thing about setting up concerts, and neither does Anders. I'm kind of overwhelmed, but I've made a decision. Instead of panicking, I'm gonna give the whole thing to God and charge at this challenge with all my heart.

I mean, everyone has to face challenges; there are overwhelming homework assignments and massive chores our parents want us to do. Whatever it is, the key is to not freak out. We just have to do our absolute best, for God, and He'll take care of the rest.

Good Night, God

Lord, I give this challenge to You. Please help me do my best. Amen.

That's my prayer. What's yours?

Ja mata!

---

2 COMMENTS:

Maddie said . . .
Just saw the show. AMAZING! Love the red, white, and blue outfit, patriotic and hip at the same time!
Posted Friday, 9:04 p.m.

Pastor Ryan said . . .
We had a *Pop Star* party at church, and everyone thought you rocked! Tell Anders we loved his TV debut. ☺
Posted Friday, 10:32 p.m.

Day 26: Brainstorm

Mood Meter: Brainstorm!

"Time to get to work," my brother said as he barged into my room this morning. The two file folders in his hands were bursting at the seams with papers. He had been up all night researching music venues in Tokyo for me and had even printed out some graphs for me to look at.

Anders loooves gathering information. He just lives for that kind of stuff.

"The Beatles got huge after their gig on the *Ed Sullivan Show*," he began. "So I was thinking; maybe we can book you on a Japanese TV show or something."

As he went on and on about the statistical possibilities, I felt relieved. My brother is one smart dude. If anyone could help me figure this challenge out, it was him.

Anders is the brain in the family. On top of being insanely disciplined, he absolutely loves learning. He got accepted to like a zillion universities, but he's holding out for his dream school, Stanford. He was devastated when he didn't get in, but he's on some kind of waiting list or something and is hoping for a miracle. I don't even know if he has a plan B. My dad and I worry about him sometimes. It's almost as if his books are his only friends. I'd much rather have the living, breathing kind.

Anyway, I'm just glad he's working this concert thing for me, because I have no clue where to begin.

"We'll start with the director of *Yookoo*," he lectured without even noticing Kenji's camera in his face. "That's one of the most popular shows in Japan right now."

As I watched the excitement on his face, I couldn't help but smile. I have one crazy cool manager.

My Heart

Listen to advice and accept instruction, and in the end you will be wise. (Proverbs 19:20)

When I was younger, I used to argue with Anders a lot. I used to totally blow him off when he gave me advice, saying, "You're not my dad!" Over the years, though, he's learned to be less bossy, and I've learned to listen. I mean, he really knows what he's talking about most of the time. We've gotten a lot closer because of that, and I've gotten a lot wiser.

Remember, wise people listen to advice.

Good Night, God

Lord, I want to be wise. Please teach me how to take advice and listen to the people who love me. Amen.

That's my prayer. What's yours?

Ja mata!

---

1 COMMENT:

Ms. Adelina said . . .

When I was young, I never listen to what my papa say. I think, *Adelina knows best!* and then I do whatever I want. Oh, how many mistakes I make that way!

Posted Saturday, 6:51 a.m.

Day 27: A New Friend

Mood Meter: Friendly

Sunday, no show, no rehearsals, no chores, nothing to do but sleep as long as I want! At least that's what I thought. So you can imagine how irritated I was when, at 7:30 in the morning, I heard Anders and my dad getting ready in the next room.

"Guys, I'm trying to sleep!" I mumbled while trying to tune out the sound of my dad's electric razor.

"You better start getting ready!" yelled my dad. "Church starts in an hour, and it might take awhile to find."

Church?! I had assumed that we were going to have church in the hotel room on our own. You know, pray together, listen to a sermon online or something. But my dad had other plans. He had asked the concierge at the hotel for directions to an English-speaking church in Tokyo and apparently found one, Grace International Fellowship. I was NOT a happy camper.

I reluctantly got ready and headed for the lobby. We walked two blocks to the nearest train station and waited a couple of minutes for the Odakyu Railway train that would take us to our destination. I was relieved to see that most of the cars were empty. During weekdays they are packed full of businessmen on their way to work, and I was in no mood to be crushed.

The church was only a couple of stops away, on the second floor of this huge skyscraper. As the congregation began singing a hymn, an usher led us to a pew about four rows from the front. The service seemed really formal so I felt a little out of place in my T-shirt and jeans. The Japanese people there didn't seem to care, though. They went out of their way to welcome us with bows, smiles, and handshakes.

Okay, here's the cool part. The church had this huge choir, about forty people or so. As they entered, I couldn't help but notice a pink-haired girl in the back of the choir, sticking out like a sore thumb. It was Atsumi, you know, from *Pop Star Challenge*!

I was waving and stuff, trying to get her attention, but wasn't sure if she noticed. Then after the service, I felt these arms wrapping around me from behind. It was her!

"You are Christian too?" she asked with a huge grin on her face. When I answered yes, she squeezed me even tighter and squealed, "I pray for Christian friend on show!"

"Me too!" I laughed as I hugged her back. By this time, my dad was in some deep conversation with a couple of American missionaries, so we began chatting away like we had known each other forever.

She told me that she usually attended the Japanese-speaking service, but once a month her choir performed for the English service. That's why I was able to see her sing today. PERFECT TIMING! Oh yeah, I also learned that she's totally into the Beatles and has every single one of their songs memorized. I thought that was pretty cool.

When it was time to go, we happily hugged again and promised to hang out more during the week.

As I followed my family through some anciently narrow streets in search of a restaurant, I grabbed my dad's hand and gave him a huge hug.

"What was that for?" he said.

"Thanks so much for dragging me to church today!" I said as I skipped on ahead.

My dad just shook his head and laughed.

My Heart

Let us not give up meeting together, as some are in the habit of doing, but let us encourage one another—and all the more as you see the Day approaching. (Hebrews 10:25)

I am so NOT complaining that my dad made me go to church today. I know I was tired and stuff, but if I hadn't gone, I might have never known that Atsumi was a Christian. Having another Christian on the show is really going to make things easier.

God wants us to go to church. That way we can meet with other Christians and encourage each other to keep strong. I mean, this world can get a little crazy sometimes; we need each other to get through.

Good Night, God

Lord, please help me be consistent with church, no matter where I am. Oh yeah, and thanks for today! Amen.

That's my prayer. What's yours?

Ja mata!

3 COMMENTS:

Maddie said . . .

Blistering bananas! I saw her on the show. That Atsumi girl can sing!

Posted Sunday, 1:08 p.m.

Sabine said . . .

We need you back desperately. Pastor Ryan led worship this morning! HELP!

Posted Sunday, 2:24 p.m.

Pastor Ryan said . . .

Hey, Sabine, I'm thinking of releasing a CD of my greatest hits. What do you think? LOL

Posted Sunday, 7:15 p.m.

D@y 28: Harajuku

Mood Meter: Hopelessly Cool

Today was an awesomely fun day, even though it didn't start out that great.

I woke up with a headache; I get those when I'm stressed. The weekend was now over, and only ten days remain until my big show. I still have absolutely no idea where I'm going to perform.

Anders, great big bro that he is, tried to calm me down. "Look," he said. "You worry about the music, and I'll worry about the location."

So while Anders scoured the city in search of a concert venue, I packed up my guitar and headed to Tama Studios. I spent about three hours alone in a rehearsal room, going over some tunes for the eight-song show. I need to have a set list by Wednesday, because my backup band needs it by then.

When I was done, I ran into Atsumi and Etienne in the hall. They were heading to Harajuku and asked if I wanted to come.

Did I want to come? That's like asking a starving kid if he wants food. OF COURSE I wanted to come. I had heard of the Harajuku shopping district in all my pop star magazines. It's one of the trendiest places on earth. If I wanted to follow Pop Star Plan Rule #31, "Hang out with the hip," then Harajuku was definitely the place to be. I even had my green tourist T-shirt on, the one with the picture of the hanging camera, perfect!

I called my dad for permission and then texted Anders to see if he wanted to hang with us. Then we jammed ourselves into a three o'clock train and blasted off.

The streets were full, I mean FULL of people our age.

We spent the afternoon walking from clothing store to clothing store, talking, and just people watching. We saw some awesome-looking vintage stuff, stuff that I've never seen back home. I ended up buying a couple of T-shirts and a long brown skirt.

Oh yeah, I made an important discovery today: Atsumi is totally CRAZY, in a good way, of course. Check this out. She talks to everyone she meets. She even went up to this band that was playing on the street and began singing "Hard Day's Night" with them. I would have been totally embarrassed, but she didn't care. It's like she's totally unafraid to be herself.

The cool thing is that she's also totally open about her faith. At one point, she asked Etienne point-blank, "Do you know Jesus? He good for your life."

I could tell Etienne didn't know how to answer. He just smiled and acted interested, even though he felt uncomfortable with the question. He would never say anything rude. He's really sweet in that way.

Anyway, Anders met up with us around dinnertime, and we headed for Atsumi's favorite noodle café.

Okay, this is where the story gets interesting. While we're there, Anders, who hardly ever talks to girls, started talking to Atsumi.

As they chatted away, Etienne and I had this cool conversation about music, movies, you know, typical stuff.

It seemed like we were there FOREVER. I mean, Atsumi and Anders were so focused on their conversation that they didn't even notice the mean looks the owner of the place was giving us. I had to actually pull Anders away from the table before the guy kicked us out of there.

Hmm . . . interesting?

My Heart

I am not ashamed of the gospel, because it is the power of God for the salvation of everyone who believes: first for the Jew, then for the Gentile. (Romans 1:16)

I totally LOVE the way Atsumi is. She is so bold about her faith. I wish I could be like that. Sometimes it's really hard for me to share about God. I worry so much about what other people are going to think about me, so I just keep God to myself most of the time. I feel bad because I know that God wants us to be brave and unashamed of who we are as Christians.

I know you probably feel that way too sometimes. When you do, ask God for courage, and remember that being one of God's kids is the coolest thing ever.

Good Night, God

Lord, help me be proud of our friendship so I can talk about You openly. Amen.

That's my prayer. What's yours?

Oh yeah, before I go, if anyone has any song ideas for my concert, let me know. I will be sooo thankful.

Ja mata!

---

3 COMMENTS:

Stephanie said . . .
You have to play your new song, "Wait." It rocks.
Posted Monday, 8:29 a.m.

Maddie said . . .
Definitely sing "Rock Lobster." Remember the time you played that at the beach and the whole youth group was dancing?
Posted Monday, 9:42 a.m.

Izzy said . . .
Don't remind me. That was totally embarrassing!
Posted Tuesday, 8:32 a.m.

Day 29: Harajuku Children's Hospital

Mood Meter: Sympathetic

Anders still hasn't found a place to play yet, and I'm reeeeeeally starting to freak out. He spent pretty much all morning and afternoon yesterday calling people up, with absolutely zero luck.

I think he's starting to stress out too. He didn't say a word to anyone at breakfast this morning; he just kept tapping his foot on the floor like a nervous rabbit. I wonder what will happen if we can't find a place for me to play. Will they just send me home automatically?

Anyway, while he was out searching today, I spent five hours in the studio working on my set. I think I have it down. I'm going to open with "Dance Town" by Energi and close with "How Can I Keep from Singing," for my mom. As for the rest, you'll just have to watch the show to find out!

When my fingers started blistering from all the strumming, I knew it was time to quit. I headed over to Atsumi's rehearsal room to see what she was up to. She was off to visit her sick sister in the hospital and asked if I wanted to keep her company. I had nothing planned, so I said yes.

We dashed across the street to the subway station and caught a train just before it left the platform.

As we rumbled along, Atsumi explained that Yakiko, her nine-year-old sister, had been in the hospital for a week. They had found something wrong with her kidneys and were doing some tests. From the look in her eyes, I could tell she was worried.

"My sister not happy," she said. "She scared."

I grabbed Atsumi's hand and gave it a squeeze. I knew exactly how it felt to have someone you love in the hospital.

We eventually got there and took the elevator to the children's ward on the twenty-first floor. There were kids everywhere. Many had IV tubes in their wrists, and some had shaved heads. Others sat solemnly in wheelchairs. Everyone looked kind of worried and serious.

When Yakiko saw Atsumi, she sat up in her bed and smiled. After being introduced to her family, I kind of stood in the back of the room as the sisters excitedly talked in Japanese.

When it was time to leave, they gave each other this massive hug. I could tell by the tears in their eyes that neither wanted their time together to end.

We didn't talk much on the ride back. I mean, there wasn't really anything to say. Atsumi was going through a hard time, and all she needed was someone to sit with her and let her cry.

I guess, today, God wanted me to be that someone.

I put my arm around her and quietly watched her tears crash on the dirty, gray subway floor.

My Heart

Rejoice with those who rejoice; mourn with those who mourn. (Romans 12:15)

I think that Atsumi just needed company, not words today. When my mom was dying, people at church would sometimes try to talk me out of my pain. I appreciated all the Bible verses and stuff they told me, but it usually didn't make me feel any better. I was just hurting too bad.

There was one thing that helped more than anything, though. One day, after group, I started bawling. Pastor Ryan and his wife, Stephanie, sat next to me. The cool thing was that they didn't say a word. They just sat and cried with me, for over an hour! When it was time to go, I felt a zillion times better. I was still hurting, but I didn't feel alone. Maybe that's why God tells us to "mourn with those who mourn."

Good Night, God

Lord, help me celebrate with the happy and cry with those who are sad. Amen.

That's my prayer. What's yours?

Ja mata!

Stephanie said . . .
Then Ryan and I went home and cried for another couple of hours. Your
     mom was like a second mother to so many of us, and our church will
     never be the same without her.
Posted Tuesday, 7:22 p.m.

Ms. Adelina said . . .
Preciosa, are you sure you are only sixteen?
Posted Tuesday, 7:25 p.m.

D@y 30: A Bright Idea

Mood Meter: Einstein Smart

A shiny, light bulb idea popped up over my head this morning! It came to me while I was in the van on the way to the studio. I have the perfect concert venue. THE HOSPITAL!

Check this out. Atsumi and I could do a concert for the children's ward. It would totally cheer the kids up and help them forget about being sick for a while. We could also make it a charity-type concert where we sell VIP seats and stuff. The hospital could use the money to make a game room or something. It would be awesome!

When I got to the studio, I flew into Atsumi's rehearsal space to tell her my idea. She was in the middle of a song with her backup band, but I didn't care.

"What happened?" she asked as she set down her electric guitar.

I took a deep breath and told her my amazing plan. By the time I was done, she was literally jumping with excitement. She had tentative plans to perform at Shinjuku Park, but she said she could easily cancel them.

We spent the next two hours discussing everything from how the stage would be set up to our outfits.

I can't wait!!

My Heart

Then the righteous will answer him, "Lord, when did we see you hungry and feed you, or thirsty and give you something to drink? When did we see you a stranger and invite you in, or needing clothes and clothe you? When did we see you sick or in prison and go to visit you?"
The King will reply, "I tell you the truth, whatever you did for one of the least of these brothers of mine, you did for me." (Matthew 25:37–40)

The best part about this whole concert thing is that we'll actually get to cheer those hospital kids up, at least for an hour or so. It will be like we're helping Jesus with our music.

Did you know that you can actually help Jesus? It's true. The Bible says that when we help people in need, it's like we're helping Him. Pretty awesome, don't you think?

Good Night, God

Lord, I really appreciate the concert idea. Please help me come up with even more ideas to help the hurting people around me. Amen. That's my prayer. What's yours?

Ja mata!

---

1 COMMENT:

Maddie said . . .

Thanks for the text. I'm glad Anders finally taught you how to SMS from Japan! Hey, maybe he can rig a massive bird mail line across the Pacific. It would be a lot cheaper (ha ha).

Posted Wednesday, 4:15 p.m.

Day 31: Moon Babies Madness

Mood Meter: Excited, I Think . . .

"Hey, sis," said Anders with a smile as he walked into the hotel restaurant for breakfast. "Guess who's playing the Tokyo Dome next Wednesday?"

"I don't know, U2?" I guessed and bit into my waffle.

"No, Moon Babies!" he shouted, practically knocking me off my seat.

"No way!" I shrieked. "They're like my favorite British band of all time."

"I know," he answered smugly. "That's why I booked YOU as their opening act!"

Okay, at this point I almost passed out. Anders had landed me an opening slot for one of the biggest bands in the universe.

This is big, totally BIG. In case you haven't heard, during the last three years, Moon Babies has sold more CDs than anyone on the planet. Just getting tickets to one of their shows is almost impossible, let alone opening for them. Apparently, Trevor Carson, their lead singer, is a huge *International Pop Star Challenge* fan. When Anders heard that, he got busy making some phone calls, and the rest is history.

I jumped up and gave Anders a huge hug. "You are the best man-ager in the history of managers!" I screamed as he tried to pry my arms away.

At this point, I remembered that my faithful sidekicks, Kenji and Miya, were there, filming away. I didn't care; I had reason to be excited. Performing my *Pop Star Challenge* concert at the Tokyo Dome, in front of thirty thousand screaming Moon Babies fans, would definitely earn me enough votes to get to the next round.

Of course, I would have to cancel the hospital show. But I think Atsumi will totally understand. I mean, come on, a chance to open for Moon Babies only comes around once every zillion years or so. She'll understand. Right?

My Heart

Make plans by seeking advice; if you wage war, obtain guidance. (Proverbs 20:18)

Okay, I'm starting to feel guilty now. I know I made a commitment, but Moon Babies, that would just be off the charts! AHHHHH! I'm so confused. The Bible says to ask for advice before making any big plans, so I'm putting it out there. What should I do?

Good Night, God

Lord, I'm not sure what I should do about this whole concert situation. Help me do what makes You smile. Amen.
That's my prayer. What's yours?
Ja mata!

---

3 COMMENTS:

Maddie said . . .
Moon Babies, definitely. Just think of all the people you can reach.
Posted Thursday, 3:17 p.m.

Pastor Ryan said . . .
The hospital gig really seemed like a good idea, Iz, but it's not a slam-dunk decision. I totally get what Maddie is saying too.
Posted Thursday, 4:24 p.m.

Ms. Adelina said . . .
Speak with God and Atsumi first, before you make the decision.
Posted Thursday 6:07 p.m.

D@y 32: Decision Day

Mood Meter: Determined

I read all your comments before heading to the studio this morning. Perfect timing. Thanks for all the advice, guys.

I had to meet Atsumi at eleven for rehearsal, which was good. I figured I could talk things over with her. You know, kind of test the waters before making any final decisions about anything. She beat me to the punch, though.

"I have good news!" she said, while running down the studio hallway. "I speak with hospital, and they very, very happy for concert!"

I tried to fake a smile as she went on. "My sister, she tell all her friends, and they very happy too."

As we headed into the rehearsal room, I was starting to feel sick, in a nervous kind of way. Just one look at Atsumi's excited smile told me that this meant a lot to her.

I didn't have the heart to even bring up the Moon Babies thing.

My Heart

Simply let your "Yes" be "Yes", and your "No," "No"; anything beyond this comes from the evil one. (Matthew 5:37)

Okay, I think I've got it. I know I didn't make any promises to Atsumi or anything, but I feel like the right thing to do is to play the hospital show. I told her I would, and I don't want to go back on my word.

It's like this. As Christians, our yes and no should be as good as a promise. I mean, if we say we're going to do something, then we should do it, promise or not. Anyway, that's what I've been thinking.

Good Night, God

Lord, help me have peace about this decision. I think I've made the right choice, but I'm not totally sure yet. Amen.

That's my prayer. What's yours?

Ja mata!

1 COMMENT:

James Baxter said . . .

I think you're doing the right thing, sweetie.

Posted Friday, 6:01 a.m.

D⍺y 33: How to Disappoint Your Manager

Mood Meter: Torn in Two

In the world of pop music, there are many ways to disappoint your manager and possibly destroy your musical career. Here are five:

1. When he amazingly books the biggest show of your career, tell him to cancel it. Get ready because he might scream, "WHAT?" and drop his bowl of Coconut Crazies on the floor.
2. Explain to your manager that you would rather play for one hundred people at a hospital instead of thirty thousand at the Tokyo Dome. When he goes into a frustrated fit and tells you how hard it was to book the show, explain that you don't want to let your Japanese friend down. At this point, he'll probably start banging his head on the table.
3. Listen as he explains the consequences of your decision: the Moon Babies, upset that you cancelled, will never let you play with them again, *International Pop Star Challenge* viewers will probably not vote you through to the next round, and your manager will quit.
4. Begin to doubt your decision as you hear about some of the other contestants' Performance Night plans. Etienne—don't ask me how—will be performing at the Budokan, where the Beatles made their Japan debut. Goth girl, Colleen, booked a gig at the Unit, which is like the most happening place in Tokyo right now. To top it off, "America, Rock and Roll!" Miklos will be performing with the Tokyo Symphony Orchestra!
5. Book me at a museum, because I'M HISTORY.

Oyasumi nasai! (That means "Good night" in Japanese. I'm totally exhausted.)

3 COMMENTS:

Pastor Ryan said . . .

"If you call out for insight and cry aloud for understanding, and if you look for it as for silver and search for it as for hidden treasure, then you will understand the fear of the Lord and find the knowledge of God" (Proverbs 2:3–5).

Don't panic, Iz. Look for God's will like you're looking for treasure. It's His opinion that matters more than anything. He'll let you know what to do.

Posted Saturday, 9:43 a.m.

Maddie said . . .

Lord, help Iz totally and completely make the right decision, one that makes You smile.

Posted Saturday, 11:46 a.m.

Sabine said . . .

Amen! (Maddie and I are hanging out right now).

Posted Saturday, 11:47 a.m.

Day 34: Pop Star Mania

Mood Meter: Dancing on Puffy White Clouds

You'll never guess who I met today! Trevor Carson!

I know, it's totally unreal. I was out on the curb, waiting for the studio van to pick me up for rehearsals, when all of a sudden this black limo pulled up. I knew it was someone famous, because all of a sudden, like thirty paparazzi photographers stampeded toward the curb where the chauffeur was letting some hip-looking guys out.

So I flattened myself against this brick wall to keep from getting crushed. Of course, being the starstruck girl that I am, I desperately tried to peek over the crowd to catch a glimpse of who it was. That's when I saw them, Moon Babies! They were staying at Sunrow Ginza, MY HOTEL!

Anyway, I stood up on this planter to get a better view, and what I saw was awesome! Hundreds of screaming fans were gathering across the street, cameras were flashing away, and TV crews were desperately trying to get the band to say something to them. It was like all my pop star dreams come to life, the real deal!

So there I was, standing on top of this wall, when I hear this familiar British voice. "Izzy Baxter? Is that you?" It was Trevor Carson, calling ME!

"No way!" I gushed, making a total fool of myself.

Trevor didn't care, though. He just laughed and told me how much he was looking forward to our concert together. Imagine, Trevor Carson looking forward to playing with ME!

As cameras flashed around me like fireflies, an incredibly clear thought rained down on me. My Pop Star Plan was working. I had dreamed of this kind of attention for years. The cameras, the crowds, THIS WAS IT!

So if I want more of this, I need to stick with the plan. Rule #5 says: "If you're not a headliner, open for someone who is." There's the answer. I'm supposed to play the Tokyo Dome.

This Tokyo Dome concert, it just feels right. I think the whole Trevor Carson meeting was probably a God thing. It's meant for me to open for Moon Babies. Besides, the hospital will always be there; the Moon Babies won't.

I know, I know. Atsumi might be a little upset at first, but she'll get

over it after a while. I mean, she'll have to.
Ja mata!

3 COMMENTS:

Ms. Adelina said . . .
Listen carefully, Preciosa. Life isn't only Izzy. Every decision you make is
not just for you. It is for you friends, it is for you family, and it is for all
the people that God put in you life.
Posted Sunday, 1:30 p.m.

Pastor Ryan said . . .
"Wounds from a friend can be trusted, but an enemy multiplies kisses"
(Proverbs 27:6).
Listen to Ms. Adelina, Iz. "Wounds from a friend can be trusted." I know it
may hurt, but I think she's right. You need to make sure you're not
trying to get what you want, at the expense of Atsumi and the kids
at the hospital who are looking forward to your show. You should
really pray about this one a little more.
Posted Sunday, 1:52 p.m.

Stephanie said . . .
Lord, it's me again. Help Iz hear Your voice in all of this. Amen.
Posted Sunday, 3:39 p.m.

Check out my latest video blog at
www.izzyspopstarplan.com/videos
and click on Day 84.

Day 35: Countdown

Mood Meter: Moved

Some days, waking up is exciting, like when it's your birthday or when you're going to spend a summer day at the beach.

On other days, though, waking up makes you feel sick inside, like when you have to tell one of your best friends that you're bailing on her. Today definitely fell into the "sick inside" category.

I was meeting Atsumi at the hospital at ten, and that's when I planned to tell her. She would be playing Wednesday night's concert alone.

As the studio van crawled downtown, I tried to convince myself, and TV viewers, that I was doing the right thing. "No one ever said that the road to pop stardom was going to be easy," I told Kenji and his camera. "I mean, I knew that there were going to be tough decisions to make; this is just one of them."

I didn't see Atsumi in the reception area, so I headed up to the children's ward to see if she was with her sister. When I got off the elevator, a little girl in a wheelchair started talking excitedly to me in Japanese. She had this massive scar on her shaved head, and I figured it was from surgery.

I couldn't understand a word she was saying, but I could tell she wanted me to come with her. She grabbed my hand and led me to the room she shared with four other patients. She smiled and started pointing at a hand-drawn picture on the wall. There, in beautiful crayon, was a girl singing. I could tell it was me because of the red, white, and blue outfit.

By the time I was done gaping at this little girl's masterpiece, I was surrounded by kids of all ages. They touched my hair, held my hands, and even asked me for my autograph.

A lot of the kids kept trying to tell me something, so I looked to one of the nurses for help. "They happy you come sing for them!" she translated in broken English.

I felt like a complete loser. Here were all these hurting kids excited to see my show, and I was about to break their hearts. WHAT WAS I THINKING?

I pried myself loose from little arms and dashed toward the door.

Atsumi and I were going to rock that hospital on Wednesday night, and we had a lot of rehearsing to do.

My Heart

If anyone has material possessions and sees his brother in need but has no pity on him, how can the love of God be in him? Dear children, let us not love with words or tongue but with actions and in truth. (1 John 3:17–18)

I felt so good leaving that hospital today. I finally made my decision, and the right decision, I might add! You know, I can't just go around saying I'm a Christian and then not do anything about it. What good is that? God wants us to care for the people around us who are hurting, even when it's not the most popular thing to do. So if I really have faith in God, I need to be doing that, right?

Good Night, God

Lord, I don't want to just talk about being a Christian. I want to LIVE like one. Amen.

That's my prayer. What's yours?

Sayonara (Bye!)

---

2 COMMENTS:

Maddie said . . .
Okay, totally ignore my Tokyo Dome advice. You definitely need to play the hospital gig.
Posted Monday, 11:01 a.m.

Pastor Ryan said . . .
It's cool how God seems to make everything clear. Isn't it? ☺
Posted Monday, 4:15 p.m.

Day 36: Sing, Sing, Sing!

Mood Meter: Lightning Bolt Energy

"I can't breathe!" I squealed in yet another fit of laughter, as Atsumi messed up another dance move.

"I not dancer." She giggled and threw an empty water bottle at me.

After eight hours of rehearsing, we had an extreme case of the giggles and were ready to call it quits. We felt confident about our set list and had worked out some cool harmonies on the two songs we planned to sing together.

I don't think I've EVER had such a good time practicing. Every dance move felt like sheer joy, and every song felt like it meant something. I mean, we weren't just singing for ourselves. We were doing it for the kids, and for God.

As we ran through one last song, I heard someone clapping at the back of the small hospital auditorium. It was Anders.

"What are you doing here?" I said, as I hopped off the stage.

"I'm your manager, aren't I?" he said.

I smiled and answered, "Yeah, I guess we're stuck with each other, bro."

It was the perfect ending to a perfect day.

My Heart

I have told you this so that my joy may be in you and that your joy may be complete. (John 15:11)

Doing the right thing doesn't always feel good at first. Sometimes it takes sacrifice and it hurts, like sacrificing my Moon Babies show. But, in the end, doing what God wants feels incredible. You get this peace in your heart, and true joy begins to bloom like a field full of daisies.

Good Night, God

Lord, help me always remember what it feels like to do the right thing. Amen.

That's my prayer. What's yours?

Oyasumi nasai!

---

2 COMMENTS:

Ms. Adelina said . . .
Remember, rest you voice tomorrow. No talking before you show!
Posted Tuesday, 7:12 a.m.

Izzy said . . .
That's like telling a fish to stop swimming, but I'll try.
Posted Tuesday, 11:23 p.m.

D@y 37: @Performance Night Japan

Mood Meter: Amplified

The big show just finished, and I'm blogging from backstage. I have soooo much to tell you!

Here's the scoop. All the contestants performed their concerts at 6:00 p.m., Japan time. A film crew was assigned to each venue. They taped a few songs and shot some backstage footage.

Overall, our concert went pretty well. I was kind of nervous at first, but when I started singing I felt pretty confident. The best part of the night was seeing the kids' faces. They seemed so excited to be part of a TV show. It was as if for one night, they could forget all about being sick, and just be kids again. Sure, it wasn't the same as performing in front of thousands at the Tokyo Dome, but it was cool in its own way.

Oh yeah, I forgot to tell you. The hospital ended up selling about fifty VIP tickets to the show and made over 5 million yen, which is a TON of money. Like, more than $50,000! They're gonna use it to build a game room. Awesome!

After the show, we got into a limo and raced over to Tama Studios for the actual *Pop Star Challenge* taping. When we got there, Renee met us at the door and rushed us to makeup. We only had about thirty minutes to get ready for the two-hour live show. Well, it's live in Japan, at least; you guys will have to wait until 8 p.m. California time to watch.

During the show, they showed footage of us getting ready for our concerts and stuff. I started busting up when they showed the conductor of the Tokyo Symphony desperately trying to get heavy metal Miklos to tone down his voice.

Then came the part of the show where the judges rate your performance. I was totally stressed when they called me out onto the stage. After watching a song from the hospital concert on the big screen, I nervously turned toward the judges' table to hear what they had to say.

Aiko was first. "You singing not the biggest," she began, "but you heart is very, very big!"

"I agree," added Marshall Phillips, "playing the hospital was a bold move. You could have played in front of thousands, but instead you went with your heart. Well done, Izzy."

Giuseppe went last, and he was the one I was really worried about. What he said could make or break a contestant. I closed my eyes and waited for the verdict.

"Isabella, Isabella," he began, "millions, they want to become famous. They all look the same, dress the same, do the same. But the world needs something different. I think the world is ready for someone like you."

So there you have it. They reeeeeally liked my performance! I think I have a shot at Paris.

Don't forget to vote tonight! Remember, you only have twenty-four hours after the show ends.

My Heart

By this all men will know that you are my disciples, if you love one another. (John 13:35)

What the judges really liked about our performance tonight was that Atsumi and I were different. We didn't just go all out for ourselves like a lot of people do in life. We actually thought about the hurting kids in the hospital and made some sacrifices to help them out.

When we love like that, people are going to notice.

Good Night, God

Lord, help people notice that we are Christians because of how we love. Amen.

That's my prayer. What's yours?

Sayonara!

---

2 COMMENTS:

Maddie said . . .
Show just ended. Gotta vote, vote, vote!!!
Posted Wednesday, 10:01 p.m.

Stephanie said . . .
One hour of voting down! Twenty-three hours left to go. ☺
Posted Wednesday, 11:00 p.m.

Day 38: @Vote Night Japan

Mood Meter: You'll see

Spoiler warning: the following blog contains the results of tonight's *Pop Star Challenge* Vote Night show. If you haven't watched yet, STOP READING NOW!

Tonight was totally nerve-racking, but it's finally over, whew! Here's what happened:

Atsumi: On her way to Paris. Yay!

Etienne: Also, on his way to Paris after an amazing acoustic gig.

Hadiya: Heading back home to Kenya after a shaky show. The nerves got to her.

Miklos: The rock king pulls it off and makes it to the next round.

Colleen: Not enough votes to move on . . . sniff, sniff. What am I going to do without my British buddy?

As for Izzy Baxter, well, I'm sad to report that . . . I won't be coming home anytime soon! Paris, here I come!

My Heart

Give, and it will be given to you. A good measure, pressed down, shaken together and running over, will be poured into your lap. For with the measure you use, it will be measured to you. (Luke 6:38)

I have to admit, there was a little pang in my heart when I stepped onto that hospital stage on Wednesday. It wasn't easy. I kept thinking of the Moon Babies show and what I was missing. But I feel like God totally blessed my decision to give. I mean, I'm so happy right now I could scream.

You know, when we give, God sees it and blesses us for it. Sure, it may not always feel good at the moment, but, in the end, you're gonna be shining like the glow-in-the-dark stars on my ceiling back home.

Good Night, God

Lord, thanks for right decisions! Amen.
That's my prayer. What's yours?
Bye, and thanks for voting!

---

3 COMMENTS:

Pastor Ryan said . . .
I voted for you so many times I can barely type. CONGRATULATIONS!
Posted Thursday, 10:02 p.m.

Ms. Adelina said . . .
Wonderful, simply wonderful.
Posted Thursday, 10:11 p.m.

Maddie said . . .
Nooooooooooo waaaaaaaaaay!
Posted Thursday, 10:42 p.m.

D⊛y 39: Rainbow Bridge

Mood Meter: Mixed, like a Smoothie

I just got back from a party on this manmade island on Tokyo Bay. The island is called Odaiba, and the only way to get there is to go across this huge, rainbow-lit bridge, scary high!

Anyway, it was a barbecue-type deal to say good-bye to the ten contestants who didn't make it through to the next round. Tragically sad, I know. There were a lot of tears. All twenty of us had been through so much together over the last few weeks, and we had bonded. It will be hard not seeing half of them anymore, especially Colleen.

After dinner, they built these huge bonfires, and we hung out on the beach. All the ups and downs of the week had taken a lot out of me, so I picked up my guitar and headed closer to the water for some alone time.

While I sat in the sand, I heard a familiar voice behind me.

"Beautiful," said Etienne, as he plopped down beside me.

"What?" I said, startled.

"The lights," he said, pointing across the bay toward Tokyo. "They're beautiful."

Luckily, it was kind of dark outside, because I was totally blushing at this point. I mean, it's not every day that a French pop star comes along and starts talking to you.

"Do you mind?" he said, as he picked up my guitar and started strumming.

"Go right ahead," I said nervously. "Play me one of your songs."

So he did. It was this really sad, sweet ballad.

Where were you in all these photographs?
Were you taking the picture, or were you far away,
Like some enchanted dream, that I could never believe in?

He told me the song was about his father.

"Work, work, and more work," he said, as he dug his feet into the sand. "That's all he does. Sometimes I feel left behind, you know, like a lost sheep."

We ended up talking for, like, an hour. He really opened up.

Now, Dad, I know what you're thinking. You don't want me hanging out alone with guys, but DON'T FREAK. There were lots of people around us the whole time.

My Heart

The LORD himself goes before you and will be with you; he will never leave you nor forsake you. Do not be afraid; do not be discouraged. (Deuteronomy 31:8)

I felt sorry for Etienne. I totally know how he feels because when my mom died, I kind of felt abandoned too. It's hard to be left alone in this world. I mean, we're just kids. We need help. But one thing I realized through my mom's sickness is that God will NEVER abandon us. Even if everyone else fails us, He'll still be there, holding our hands.

So smile. You are not alone!

Good Night, God

Lord, help us always know that You're there. No matter what we're going through. Amen.

That's my prayer. What's yours?

Sayonara!

---

3 COMMENTS:

James Baxter said . . .
Be careful, sweetie.
Posted Friday, 10:00 a.m.

Izzy said . . .
I know, Dad. I'm not a baby anymore.
Posted Friday 10:31 a.m.

James Baxter said . . .
You'll always be my baby.
Posted Friday, 11:04 a.m.

Day 40: Good-bye, Tokyo!

Mood Meter: Roller-Coaster Thrilled

I'm on my way to Paris right now. Internet on the plane, crazy cool! Here's the FYI on my day:

One argument with Anders over who gets the window seat on the plane.

Two bags of sour ropes, completely devoured.

Three fashion magazines read from cover to cover.

Four completed levels of my *Manga Bear* video game.

Five trips to the same airport gift shop.

SIX HOURS WAITING TO BOARD MY DELAYED FLIGHT TO PARIS!

My Heart

"I have come that they may have life, and have it to the full." (John 10:10)

I hate waiting around in airports. I mean, you just sit there trying to entertain yourself until your flight leaves. Not fun!

While I was aimlessly sitting at the gate today, a sad thought came to me. A lot of people are living their *lives* as if they are in some big waiting room. They just go through their days, trying to entertain themselves until it's time to, well, die, I guess.

But life is WAY more than a waiting room. God has an amazing life planned out for all of us, on earth and in heaven. We just have to follow *His* plans.

Good Night, God

Lord, help us live life to the full, the way You meant it to be. Amen.
That's my prayer. What's yours?
L8R

---

1 COMMENT:

Ms. Adelina said . . .
Travel safely, Preciosa.
Posted Saturday, 8:13 a.m.

PART 3

Blinded by the City of Lights

Can you lift me up, high above this silence
Where you fill the air
With a million songs of grace?

"SING"—IZZY BAXTER

Day 41: Bienvenue!

Mood Meter: Wow!

We touched down bright and early this morning. *Getting* to Paris was pretty boring, as eleven-hour flights usually are, but *arriving* in Paris, well, that was anything but. As we pulled up to the gate at Charles de Gaulle Airport, I unbuckled and stood up to get my backpack out of the overhead compartment. That's when the show's publicist, Renee, motioned for me to sit down from across the aisle.

"Why can't we leave?" I asked Christine, who had been sitting next to me during the flight.

"Oh, my dear little inexperienced one," said the ultra hip stylist as she patted my hand. "In Paris we always wait until all the passengers deplane before exiting."

"That's weird," I said as I plopped back down into my seat. "Why do we do that?"

"Oh, you'll see," she said with a mischievous grin on her face.

I had no idea what she was talking about, but I was about to find out. After the "regular" passengers left, the ten *Pop Star Challenge* survivors were ready to make their French debut. As we grabbed our stuff and headed down the tunnel toward the terminal, I was completely unaware of the madness to come.

PAPARAZZI! At least fifty of them crushed toward us like a tidal wave. Cameras flashed and microphones flew into our faces while reporters shouted questions in broken English. Luckily, an army of security guards cleared the way for us as we headed toward the limos waiting to take us to our hotel.

Christine laughed as she shoved me into the first limo in line. "The show is HUGE here in France," she told me, as she made a hopeless attempt to straighten my frazzled hair. "*International Pop Star Challenge* has hit number one in fourteen countries now, so get used to the attention."

As we pulled onto the French highway, I worried about Anders and Dad. In all the chaos, we had gotten separated. Craning my neck to see if Dad and Anders had gotten into a limo safely, I saw something that blew my mind. Plastered on the side of an office building was a fifty-foot advertisement featuring someone I was starting to get to know pretty well, ETIENNE ROUSSEAU!

I took a deep breath, sat back in my seat, and stared out the window. For the entire hour it took to get to our downtown hotel, only one thought kept spinning through my head, *This is going to be crazy—crazy cool!*

My Heart

For where your treasure is, there your heart will be also.
(Matthew 6:21)

On one hand, I absolutely loved all the attention today. I mean come on, the paparazzi, the French fans screaming for my autograph, the flashbulbs flashing in my face—it was a dream come true. But then, on the other hand, I feel kind of confused. Should I be liking this so much? Am I *treasuring* this too much? The Bible says that what we are really, totally into, what we dream about, crave, go all out for, that's where our heart is. So I guess the question I'm asking is, where's my heart?

Good Night, God

Lord, help me treasure what You treasure. Then my heart will be in the right place. Amen.
That's my prayer. What's yours?
L8R

3 COMMENTS:

Pastor Ryan said . . .
You're asking the right questions, Iz. I'm proud of you.
Posted Sunday, 1:07 p.m.

Izzy said . . .
Must be your great lessons. You taught me well, wise one.
Posted Sunday, 2:34 p.m.

Stephanie said . . .
Oh no! All those compliments are going to his head. Pretty soon he won't be able to fit through our front door.
Posted Sunday, 9:45 p.m.

Day 42: I Could Get Used to This

Mood Meter: Tops

Okay, so I'm into some pretty serious pop star territory over here in France. It's been unbelievable! Check this out.

Since my body clock is still ticking Tokyo time, I got up waaay too early this morning. With my family still asleep, I headed downstairs to tour our new home for the next three weeks, the Hotel Georges Pompidou. Sound impressive? Well, it totally is! Beautifully ancient, classy, and probably the most awesomely elegant hotel I'll ever stay in for my entire life.

Anyway, as the elevator doors opened at the ground floor, flash-bulbs sent my morning eyes into shock. Paparazzi! In a bit of a panic, I nervously smiled and headed off toward this huge fountain in the atrium area. Dumb idea. The frantic photographers smelled blood and began following me like hungry mosquitoes.

Adding to the insanity, a crowd of about twenty hotel guests began clamoring to get a glimpse of the action. Some waved notepads in front of me, wanting my autograph. Even though I've dreamed of this kind of attention, now that I had it, it kind of freaked me out. I mean, I really started to worry about my safety.

Within a minute, a familiar arm reached into the madness and plucked me out. It was Christine, and she was laughing. "Izzy, Izzy, Izzy," she playfully scolded, confidently dragging me away from the chaos and through an Employees Only exit. "You are a pop star now, my dear. No more makeup-free morning strolls to the lobby, or ANYWHERE, for that matter."

I followed her down a hall and into a banquet room marked *International Pop Star Challenge* Wardrobe. I plopped down onto the makeup chair, and Christine began to work her wonders. "A little blush—not too much, though," she mumbled to herself. "Lipstick is a must. Natural colors, of course, to complement your high cheek-bones." Looking into the mirror, she began to lecture. "You are in the big leagues now, missy. Unless you want to appear on the cover of *STYLE* magazine looking like some shell-shocked poseur, you'll need to start watching where you go, what you say, and most importantly, what you *wear*."

With that she pulled out three large black shopping bags from behind the mirror. "For you," she said with a huge smile on her face.

I rummaged through the bags like a kid on Christmas morning and out came the most awesome and expensive-looking clothes I have ever seen. There were funky, billowy tops and totally unique-looking leggings and skirts. And the shoes, oh the shoes! This flip-flop-wearing girl is falling in love with high-heeled shoes!

"It's who you are," said the twenty-three-year-old fashion guru as I stared dumbfounded at the $700 price tag that hung from the back of a pair of designer jeans. Maddie and Sabine, you would have loved the pockets. I was speechless.

After giving her this massive hug, I spent the next hour or so trying on my new treasures. Each and every one fit perfectly! As I modeled my new wardrobe in front of the mirror, I couldn't believe what I was seeing.

I was looking at a pop star, and that pop star was me!

My Heart
Sorry, guys. Bible verse will have to wait. I reeeeeally have to get to bed. Up early for rehearsals. Challenge Night on Friday!
L8R

5 COMMENTS:

Ms. Adelina said . . .
"What good is it for a man to gain the whole world, and yet lose or forfeit his very self?" (Luke 9:25).
Preciosa, always remember that you are much more than jewels and $700 jeans, much, much more!
Posted Monday, 10:11 a.m.

Pastor Ryan said . . .
Lord, thanks for the blessings You've given Iz. Help her always remember where those blessings came from. Amen.
Posted Monday, 2:32 p.m.

Maddie said . . .
Hey, friend, I'm almost done with the outfit design I've been working on for you. I'll e-mail it when I finish. Should I e-mail it to Christine too?
Posted Monday, 4:15 p.m.

Izzy said . . .
Um, I kind of have all the clothes I need right now. Christine's been taking care of all the wardrobe stuff for me. Thanks, though.
Posted Monday, 5:11 p.m.

Maddie said . . .
Okay. I guess.
Posted Monday, 5:21 p.m.

Day 43: Getting Artsy

Mood Meter: Can Someone Please Carry Me Back to the Hotel?

Can you believe it? Three days in Paris, and I'm falling in love—with the city, I mean. Beautifully romantic. Sigh . . .

We haven't toured any of the sights yet. I've seen the Eiffel Tower a couple of times, but from far away. I can't wait to see it up close.

Nope, no sightseeing for us busy pop stars. Instead of blissfully wandering the streets of Paris, we've been cooped up in this old warehouse all day. Nine hours of rehearsal! Totally insane. We're working on this artsy group number for Challenge Night. I can't even begin to describe it to you. It's opera meets techno-infused heavy metal. Pretty bizarre. I'm going to be wearing wings and, get this, a SILVER wig.

I can handle the song and even the weird costumes, but the choreography is killing me. It's killing all of us. Werner, the director, hired this famous French choreographer, Gerard Lafontaine, for the piece, and he's an ultra perfectionist. I think he has the whole number worked out perfectly in his head, but it's in HIS head, not OURS. That skinny little man in black drove me crazy, stopping us in the middle of the song and frantically saying things like, "Feeling, feeling, from the fear and pain within!"

I had no idea what he was talking about, and from the look on everyone's face, no one else did either. Every time Atsumi was dancing behind me, I could hear her whispering, "Remember, Izzy, from the fear and pain within!" It took every ounce of energy to keep ourselves from falling onto the floor in a giant pile of laughter.

Every once in a while, Gerard would flip out completely and storm out of the room. That left the rest of us twiddling our thumbs for hours on end as Werner and Renee tried to get him to come back.

The day wasn't all bad, though. During one of Lafontaine's meltdowns, I got to talk with Etienne for a while. Like always, he was sooooooo cool. We picked up right where we left off in Tokyo. By the way, did you know that one of the songs he performed in Japan is the number one download in Europe?! We talked about a bunch of stuff, but mostly music, of course. I asked why a big pop star like him would even want to sign up for a show like this, and he explained that he wanted his music to be heard in other countries, not just France. From the way things look, his plan is working perfectly.

Anyway, talking to him was the best forty-seven minutes I've had since arriving in Paris.

My Heart
Do not be yoked together with unbelievers. For what do righteousness and wickedness have in common? Or what fellowship can light have with darkness? (2 Corinthians 6:14)

Okay, I'm getting a bit confused here. I am reeeeeally starting to like my talks with Etienne. In fact, I'm starting to think more about him these days than anything else. I mean, what sixteen-year-old wouldn't? He doesn't just talk about himself all the time and seems really interested in my life. We totally like the same things, well, apart from God, I mean. I guess that's why I'm confused. Am I supposed to be feeling this way? Any help would be appreciated.

Good Night, God
Lord, help these confusing thoughts be, well, not so confusing. Amen.

That's my prayer. What's yours?

á bientot! (French for L8R)

---

2 COMMENTS:

Pastor Ryan said . . .
In answer to your question, I guess it all depends. Do you like him like a friend, or are you talking Paris romance here? Etienne sounds like a really neat guy, and it's okay to be friends, but you really need to be careful. He doesn't seem to have a relationship with God like you do. A boyfriend/girlfriend relationship is a *majorly* serious thing, and that definitely needs to be built on faith. Anyway, I'm preaching now. Sorry, it's my job.
Posted Tuesday, 1:32 p.m.

Ms. Adelina said . . .
Lord, help my preciosa, Izzy, always choose You first. In every way she go. Amen.
Posted Tuesday, 3:24 p.m.

D@y 44: Crush?

Only two rehearsals left until the Challenge Night show, and things are going well with the whole group song thing. Well, the part where Miklos swoops down onto the stage with these silver bird wings looks pretty dumb, but the rest of the choreography actually rocks. I guess I'm starting to understand the way Gerard Lafontaine's mind works. Now, THAT'S a scary thought, isn't it?

The clocks were barely moving until about noon, but then things started to get interesting. Atsumi and I had just collapsed onto the stage floor after our final run-through. In sympathy for my aching feet, I sat up and began massaging my toes. That's when, out of the blue, Etienne walked over and crashed down next to us. "Is my American angel getting tired?" he said as he started—get this—rubbing my shoulders. He must have seen me turn bright apple red because he stopped after just a few seconds.

I felt like a total dork because all I managed to croak out was, "Yeah, tired," as he hopped up and headed backstage.

Hold on. It gets even better. A few minutes later, as I headed toward one of the limos, Christine came running up to me with MAJOR news. "Guess what I have in my hands?" she asked, completely out of breath after trying to catch up.

Before I could answer, she handed me a black envelope. "It's an invitation to Emile Desalle's perfume launch party!" she exclaimed. "It's the hottest party in Paris, and we've been invited!"

"I'm not sure," I answered hesitantly, knowing I would have to ask my dad first.

"Etienne will be there," she teased as she pulled some lipstick from her purse.

"So?" I answered defensively, embarrassed that she seemed to know exactly what I was thinking.

"Oh, come on," she continued. "I've seen the way you've been looking at him. You're crushing big time, girl!"

That last comment threw me for a loop. Does Christine know more about my feelings than I do?

Now I definitely have a lot of thinking to do.

á bientot!

3 COMMENTS:

Stephanie said . . .

I totally know the schedule over there must be craaaaazy, but don't forget
to keep praying. That way you won't end up messing up the plans God
has for you, which, by the way, seem pretty incredible so far.
Posted Wednesday, 3:32 p.m.

Sabine said . . .

God, please help Iz sort through the messy feelings going on in her
heart right now. Amen.
Posted Wednesday, 4:22 p.m.

Anders said . . .

Here's your verse for the night, sis. It's Matthew 26:41: "Watch and pray
so that you will not fall into temptation. The spirit is willing, but the
body is weak."
Posted Wednesday, 11:20 p.m.

D@y 45: Three, Two, One, LAUNCH!

Mood Meter: Sparkly Like a Star

Who's that girl hanging with all those stars? You know, the one over by the pool with Cassidy Danes, Eric Dunst, and Trevor Carson, who, by the way, is not upset at her for ditching the Moon Babies gig. Why, could it be? Yes, it is. It's IZZY BAXTER!!!

I'm sorry. I don't mean to sound stuck-up or anything. In fact, I did feel kind of out of place at Emile Desalle's party with all those A-list stars around, at least for the first few minutes. The only thing that kept me from looking like a total loser was that I was wearing this over-the-top Giorgio Bouvier dress. It was pink silk with pearl accents around the middle and on the sleeves. I mean, do you know how much those things cost? Over a couple of thousand dollars, at least! When Christine brought it to my room after dinner, I was in total shock.

"Compliments of *Pop Star Challenge*," she said as she tossed it on my bed.

I have NEVER felt more beautiful in all my life.

The party was at Emile's estate, which is about forty minutes outside Paris. His new perfume is called Wing, so the entire place was decorated with thousands of paper birds. Some had candles in them, really cool.

Pop Star Plan Rule #22 says, "If you get a chance to hang with the stars, shine brightly." So tonight I tried my best to shine. From the moment I stepped out of the limo, I smiled as if I belonged at that gathering of beautiful people, and you know what? IT WORKED! I got to talk to so many celebrities, and, amazingly, many of them knew me!

Atsumi wasn't there since her parents wouldn't let her go, so I hung out with Christine, who had promised my dad she'd look out for me. Etienne was there as well, but he was surrounded by people so I barely got to talk to him. I did get to talk to "America, Rock and Roll" Miklos, though. He was dressed in a heavy-metal T-shirt and jeans and looked completely out of place.

"I like museeec," he said, waving his hands around the room in disgust. "Theese is nothing about the museeec." I didn't get why he was so upset. I mean, the whole night was beautiful. It really was. There were great conversations going on. There were beautiful people everywhere. Everyone seemed so happy.

You know, despite what Miklos said, I could totally see myself getting into this.

Gotta catch some zzz's now. Challenge Night tomorrow!

á bientot!

---

1 COMMENT:

Ms. Adelina said . . .
"Be happy, young man, while you are young, and let your heart give you joy in the days of your youth. Follow the ways of your heart and whatever your eyes see, but know that for all these things God will bring you to judgment" (Ecclesiastes 11:9).

Enjoy this life while you are young, Preciosa, but always remember that God watches. He watches when you are on stage, when you are at the parties, when you are falling in love. He is hoping you will do what is right.

Padre Dios, may You always shine more brightly to Izzy than any other star. Amen.
Posted Thursday, 5:15 p.m.

D@y 46: Challenge Night Paris!

Mood Meter: Messy

In five hours and twenty-five minutes, you, my West Coast friends, will be able to watch on TV what I just experienced live, Challenge Night Paris. If you haven't seen the show yet and want to be surprised, LOG OFF NOW.

The show actually kind of snuck up on me. I mean, I've been so enthralled by this "pop star" life that the music has kind of taken a backseat all week.

As I pulled up to L'Olympia, the concert hall where the Paris shows are being taped, I tried to remember the lyrics to the opening number and, to my horror, COULDN'T! I calmed myself down backstage by flipping through my Pop Star Plan journal and saying a little prayer. Thankfully, by the time the lights went dim, and Sean Moore opened with his trademark words, "Welcome to *International Pop Star Challenge*, the show that makes all your pop star dreams come true," I was good to go.

We opened with the group number, and, amazingly, got through it in one piece. My verses with German singer Edina Hayner went well, at least I thought so. I couldn't help but look good next to Edi. Man, that twenty-three-year-old can sing!

Okay, I have to admit; at first, I thought that Lafontaine's choreography was pretty dumb. Come on, wings? But after watching the number on tape afterward, I thought it was, well, dazzlingly beautiful. I think Miklos had a lot to do with that. As he sang his lines, there was pure joy written all over his face. I love watching him do his stuff. You can tell he's not in it for the fame or the money. That Bosnian boy just wants to *sing*.

My face, on the other hand, told a different story. Before the judges came out to announce our Paris challenge, they showed highlights of our first week in Paris. I was shocked at how stressed I looked. I was smiling a lot, but even in the shots of me rubbing elbows with all those celebrities at the launch party, I looked, well, worried.

Hey, the camera doesn't lie. I am stressed. There are all these conflicting feelings spinning around in my head. I do love the whole pop star vibe, but then again, do I love it too much? And then there's Etienne. Am I starting to crush on the guy? I mean, almost every clip showed me and him talking together like two love birds. It's as if the cameras know what I'm thinking or something.

After the lights came back on, the ten of us sat on these metal stools and awaited our next challenge. It was Giuseppe Rossi's turn to announce the challenge this time. In dramatic fashion, he slowly opened the envelope and began to speak.

"Paris is not only the city of lights," he preached. "It is the city of romance as well. Throughout the ages many have found love under the watchful gaze of the Eiffel Tower."

Marshall Phillips stepped in next, "A boy. A girl. A simple yet complex formula." I didn't like where this was going and began to squirm in my seat. "In this week's challenge, our talented finalists will be paired up, one male, one female. Their job will be to perform a romantic ballad under the Eiffel Tower. Will they find success or heartbreak in the city of lights?"

As Aiko Mae began to announce our performance pairings, my hands began to shake. It was Atsumi's turn first. "Atsumi Takenaga, you will join Miklos Szabo!" she said as she motioned for the two to come center stage. Applause rang out as Miklos and my smiling Japanese bud hugged in front of the cameras.

I was up next. I looked down, as the beautiful Asian revealed my destiny. "Izzy Baxter, you will grace the stage with . . ." She paused dramatically. "Etienne Rousseau."

As Etienne and I gave the expected hug on stage, one word flashed repeatedly through my teenage brain.

HELP!

2 COMMENTS:

Sabine said . . .

Here's a verse straight from my bedroom wall to you. It's Psalm 23:1–2:
"The Lord is my shepherd, I shall not be in want. He makes me lie down in green pastures, he leads me beside quiet waters."

Last night I started staring at the picture on my wall, the one of Jesus holding a little lamb, and remembered something. God is my shepherd, and He's gonna take care of me when I can't see the road up ahead. He's gonna take care of you too, Iz. He'll lead us somewhere good and peaceful. Remember that, friend.

Posted Friday, 7:15 p.m.

Stephanie said . . .

Lord, keep us safe and calm when we can't see what's up ahead. Amen.

Posted Friday, 8:11 p.m.

D@y 47: The Plot Thickens

Mood Meter: Shaken

Okay, the warm, fuzzy feelings of crushiness are getting old. I want my normal emotions back, NOW! Things are just too much for me to handle.

Here's the deal. Today was Saturday. Now that Challenge Night is over, you would think that Werner would give us a day off. But did he? No way. We had to be at the studios at eight in the morning in order to go over our song choices.

When I got to our assigned practice room, Etienne was already at the piano going over the list of romantic ballads our dear director had given us. "Any ideas?" I asked as I plopped myself on the bench next to him.

"I think, yes," he said and began singing a song I had never heard before.

> *The swirling colors they paint the night,*
> *And you're by my side.*

I listened to the melody and tried to sing the next verse.

> *We left our burdens,*
> *We left all our fear,*
> *In love we hide.*

The song was beautiful, and I instantly knew it was the one. We lost ourselves in the music for the next three hours until Renee popped her head into the room. We were late for a production meeting.

This is where things get confusing. As we walked down the hall toward the conference room, Etienne asked me, "You like coffee, no?"

Dumb me, I didn't realize where this conversation was going and answered, "Iced coffee. I practically live on the stuff when I'm back home."

So then he tells me about this great café along the banks of the Seine River that serves the best coffee in France. He said he would take me there after rehearsal one night . . . if I wanted.

I couldn't believe what I was hearing. He was asking me out!

At least that's what it sounded like. I was flattered, thrilled, and DESPERATELY DISAPPOINTED! You see, I don't know if I've told you yet, but my dad has this set-in-cement "no dating until eighteen" policy. He'll bend on a lot rules, but not that one. Believe me, I've tried. I begged and begged for him to let me go to the freshman dance with Maddie's friend Tyler last year, to no avail.

So instead of joyfully spending my Paris nights on romantic dates with the most popular teen in France, I'll be stuck in my hotel room blogging away my sorrows. Sigh.

My Heart

Children, obey your parents in the Lord, for this is right. "Honor your father and mother"—which is the first commandment with a promise—"that it may go well with you and that you may enjoy long life on the earth." (Ephesians 6:1–3)

I don't really agree with Dad's "no dating" rule. A lot of my friends can date, and they're Christians. I mean, I think I'm mature enough to handle a simple cup of coffee with a boy. But my nagging heart keeps telling me that I need to obey my dad anyway.

I guess this verse just confirms what my heart's been telling me. God wants us to obey our parents, whether we agree with them or not, "for this is right."

Good Night, God

Hey, Lord, this whole "no dating" rule is frustrating me. Please help me obey my dad, even though every ounce of me wants to do otherwise. Amen.

That's my prayer. What's yours?

L8R

4 COMMENTS:

Pastor Ryan said . . .
It hurts to do what's right sometimes. Doesn't it?
Posted Saturday, 11:32 a.m.

Izzy said . . .
No kidding. I think the whole no-dating rule is a little old-fashioned, don't you?
Posted Saturday 12:43 p.m.

Pastor Ryan said . . .
I'm sure your dad has his reasons. Talk to him about it.
Posted Saturday, 1:02 p.m.

Izzy said . . .
I would if I could. That guy has been so busy with this Web project that I barely see him. He doesn't even read my blogs anymore.
Posted Saturday, 10:45 p.m.

D@y 48: Conversation #1

Mood Meter: Perplexed

It was Sunday today, and, miracle of miracles, Werner gave us the day off. We couldn't find an English-speaking church near our hotel, so Anders and I had church in our room. We read a couple of verses and prayed for about fifteen minutes, while Dad tried to get over this miserable virus he caught over here. On top of being sick, he's been crazy busy, and I miss him. I'm going to miss him even more when he heads back to Los Angeles in a week. He has some meetings and stuff he has to go to. He was pretty stressed about leaving us alone until Anders promised to look out for me while he was gone. Oh well, at least I have my bro and Coco the stuffed monkey to hang with.

Nothing really exciting happened today. Oh yeah, I did have a conversation with Christine about my date predicament. I ran into her in the workers' hallway while I was zigzagging my way back from breakfast.

"Hey, I heard Etienne finally asked you," she said with her trade-mark smile.

"Asked me what?" I said, curious as to how she would know about Etienne asking me out.

"To coffee," she said as we darted into the workers' elevator before a couple of paparazzi waiting outside a glass door could get a clear shot.

"Yeah, but I can't go. My dad thinks I'm too young to date," I said, shaking my head in disgust.

"Wait a second," she answered, grabbing my arm like a school-teacher. "Etienne is one of the biggest names in music right now. Do you realize what a simple cup of coffee with him would do for your career?"

As we reached our floor, I searched for my key and for something to say, but the words wouldn't come. "It's a simple cup of coffee, Izzy, *not* a date," pleaded Christine. "It's just two friends hanging out. Don't tell me you are going to follow some old-fashioned rule rather than your heart. You're bigger than that, Iz."

Her words stuck in my head for the rest of the afternoon. Maybe I should be following my heart rather than my head.

Ms. Adelina said . . .

"Trust in the Lord with all your heart and lean not on your own understanding; in all your ways acknowledge him, and he will make your paths straight" (Proverbs 3:5–6).

Posted Sunday, 4:32 p.m

Pastor Ryan said . . .

Iz, the heart often speaks loudest, but that doesn't mean it's always right. Our own "understanding"' of things can't always be trusted. Trust God instead.

Posted Sunday, 4:52 p.m

Stephanie said . . .

God, help Izzy's heart be full of Your wisdom. Amen.

Posted Sunday, 5:23 p.m.

Day 49: Conversation #2

Mood Meter: Perplexed x 100

An alarming fact woke me up at five this morning: I'm totally unprepared for Performance Night! I need to get my act together and focus on the plan. Pop Star Plan Rule #41 says, "Leave your stress at the door, and focus on the music." So today I did.

I got to the studio early and diligently began working on my vocals. When Etienne walked in about an hour later, we ran through the song like pros. That's what we are, right? Professionals? We finished about noon, because he had to go to a photo shoot, and I had to go . . . well, nowhere. He gave me a quick hug and jogged to his limo.

Before getting in, he turned. "Coffee is waiting," he called. "Maybe we go, no?"

"Maybe," I answered, as my face turned a deep red.

On the lonely drive back to the hotel, I started convincing myself that Christine might be right. Maybe it wasn't a date. Maybe we could just hang for a while, and, you know, just talk.

But then Anders came along and spoiled everything. He was working on his laptop when I got back to our room. With my heart in a mess, I really needed to talk. Since Atsumi was busy shooting some Japanese commercial, Anders was the only one around to spill my guts to.

"Hey, big brother, I'm thinking of going to coffee with Etienne this week," I started, wondering how he would react.

"Dad's gonna freak," he answered calmly without even looking up from the screen.

"It's not really a date. I mean, it'll just be like going to LuLu's with Maddie," I countered.

"Iz, think about it, alone with a boy, a boy you have an obvious crush on, at a café. That sounds like a date to me." By this time he was looking at me and had a concerned look on his face.

I started getting upset. "Dad's rule is so stupid anyway. I mean, I'm sixteen. I'm traveling the world. I'm not a baby anymore!"

Anders, amazingly calm after my rant, answered, "It's not just about Dad, Izzy. Where's God in all this? Does Etienne even believe in God? Go to church? Anything?"

Something about that comment made me flip. "Why am I even talking to you?" I yelled, as I got up from the bed. "Look at me! I'm getting dating advice from someone who has never even *gone* on a date. I'm sorry, but I'm not gonna waste my entire life alone in front of a laptop like you."

I never should have said what I said. I could tell that Anders was hurt. He didn't say anything; he just picked up his laptop and headed out the door.

Now, on top of a "date" dilemma, I have an "Izzy's big mouth" dilemma to deal with.

Paris stinks.

---

4 COMMENTS:

Ms. Adelina said . . .
"All kinds of animals, birds, reptiles and creatures of the sea are being tamed and have been tamed by man, but no man can tame the tongue. It is a restless evil, full of deadly poison" (James 3:7–8).
Posted Monday, 8:32 p.m.

Stephanie said . . .
Lord, we all say things we don't mean. Help tame our tongues so that only good things come from them. Amen.
Posted Monday, 9:15 p.m.

Maddie said . . .
Okay, the Izzy I know and love would never have said something mean like that. What's been going on with you lately?
Posted Monday, 9:32 p.m.

Pastor Ryan said . . .
First of all, I hope you realize what a great brother you have, a brother who is going to make an awesome husband one day. (Are you reading this, Anders?) Second, Izzy, know that we're praying you through.
Posted Monday, 10:15 p.m.

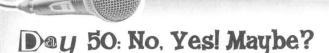

D⊚y 50: No, Yes! Maybe?

Mood Meter: Resolved

Okay, soooo much has happened in the last twenty-four hours.

First off, I got to go to a real-life movie premiere tonight! All the *Pop Star Challenge* contestants were invited. It was for *Give and Take* with Cassidy Danes and Edison Carnes. Of course, they were both there. Yay!

Christine, Atsumi, and I shared a limo and pulled up to the theater at about six. I'm glad we got there early because it took us FOREVER to walk in. Once again, Renee made sure we arrived in style. Atsumi was wearing this classy long, blue dress with a diamond necklace, while I wore this vintage, sixties-style white dress that totally screamed Izzy. The dress was sleeveless, so I was freezing from the minute I stepped out of the car, but I didn't mind because I felt like a total movie star.

There was this long, red carpet leading up to the entrance with all these camera crews and photographers piled up alongside. From the moment we got out of the car, reporters were shouting our names, hoping to get an interview. Every few steps I would stop at one of the microphones and answer some random reporter's questions. It was pretty pop star-ish.

Question: "How do you like Paris?" Answer: "It's beautiful." SMILE.

Question: "Do you think you have a chance to win?" Answer: "I don't know. There are some pretty good singers this season." SMILE.

Question: "Are you and Etienne romantically involved?" Answer: "Uh . . . no! I mean, I don't . . ." Lucky for me, Christine grabbed my arm and whisked me into the theater. It was time for the movie to start, and not a second too soon.

I spent the entire movie thinking about Etienne. The ball was in my court. If I say no to Etienne's offer, he would think I'm rejecting him. I like Etienne, *really* like him, so obviously I don't want him to feel that way. But, then again, if I say yes, I'd be going against my dad's no dating rule. I don't want to do that either. AAAAAAAHHHHHH!

By this time, I had totally lost track of what was happening on the screen, so I headed downstairs to the lobby to grab a dessert from the catering tables they had out there. I was wearing these super high heels, which was dumb because I'm a total klutz. In perfect Izzy style, I tumbled down the last four steps and landed with a *thud* on the lobby floor.

I hit the tiled floor pretty hard, but that was the least of my worries. As I looked up, I saw Etienne, sitting DIRECTLY IN FRONT OF ME! Epic embarrassment! I tried to get up quickly, as if it were no big deal, but I couldn't. My knees were banged up pretty bad, and one of my elbows was bleeding. All I could think was, *Whatever you do, don't get blood on this expensive, and borrowed, dress!* Before I knew it, I felt Etienne's warm hands helping me up.

"Your arm looks not so good," he said, as he gently guided me to a fancy red sofa. "I get you something."

Waiting for him to get back, I was in awe. Most of the guys I know back home would have totally laughed at my clumsy calamity, but not him. He was just so awesomely different.

"Here you go," he said sweetly as he returned with an armful of Band-Aids and napkins. "First, we take care of the arm."

I couldn't help but stare at him as he poured some water on a napkin and began dabbing my bleeding elbow with it. As he softly grabbed my wrist to position my arm better, I quietly spoke the word I had been wanting to say all week. "Yes."

"Yes what?" He laughed as he let go of my arm and looked at my flushed face.

"Yes, I'll go out . . . I mean, I'll have coffee with you."

"Tomorrow then." He smiled as he stuck a Band-Aid on my arm.

So there you have it. Tomorrow I'm having coffee with Etienne. I know, I know. You're all thinking, *What's your dad gonna say?* Well, first of all, my dad doesn't have to *say* anything. He's been so over-the-top busy lately, he doesn't even look at my blog anymore. Furthermore, my dad's rule is "no dating." A cup of coffee with a friend doesn't technically qualify as a *date*. So I think I'm okay there.

Most importantly, something just *feels* incredibly right about the whole thing. I know that if I just follow my heart, it'll all work out. Won't it?

3 COMMENTS:

Ms. Adelina said . . .
"There is a way that seems right to a man, but in the end it leads to death" (Proverbs 14:12).
I know your heart cries out for love, Preciosa, but don't forget to listen to God. He knows where love is.
Posted Tuesday, 6:02 p.m.

Stephanie said . . .
Lord, my heart has often led me astray. Please help our hearts lead us to where You are. Amen.
Posted Tuesday, 6:23 p.m.

Sabine said . . .
Okay, Maddie and I have been talking. Etienne, totally cool guy. You going out with him behind your dad's back, not cool at all.
Posted Tuesday, 7:12 p.m.

D@y 51: Sigh . . .

Mood Meter: Alive

I'm still in a total daze, so please forgive me if this blog seems confusing.

Tonight was the night. I actually got to spend one-on-one time with Etienne, in Paris! It was incredibly incredible. I felt like I was in a movie or something.

Where to begin, where to begin . . .

Okay, after rehearsals, which lasted until about five, I went back to the hotel to have dinner and get ready. I was too nervous to eat much, but I tried. I think Anders could tell something was up, but he kept quiet. Since our argument the other day, we haven't really talked much.

I was meeting Etienne at eight, at this off-the-wall Paris café. He said he'd never seen any paparazzi there, so I figured we would be fine. I chose to wear my sunglasses anyway, just in case.

Hoping that my dad wouldn't ask a lot of questions, I yelled a quick good-bye and headed for the door.

"Atsumi finally free tonight?" he asked, thinking I was going to hang with her.

"Yeah," I said nervously, as I put on my sunglasses and headed out the door.

Waiting for the limo in the chilly, autumn air gave me too much time to think. Guilt began descending on me like the Paris fog. But it's not like I lied or anything, Atsumi *was* free tonight. She had even called me to see if I wanted to hang out. I never actually *told* my dad that I was hanging out with her. He just believed that on his own.

The guilt flew away like a hummingbird, though, when I finally met up with Etienne. He was sitting at a corner table, next to a window with a view of the River Seine. With a warm smile, he got up, gave me a quick hug, and pulled a chair out for me. There was a cup of iced coffee waiting for me on the table, not easy to find in Paris. Wow, he actually remembered what I told him.

For the first few minutes, it was totally awkward trying to think of things to say, but then it wasn't anymore. Suddenly, it felt like we were just best buds hanging out.

"How is the injured wing?" he asked.

"Still a little sore," I answered with a smile, "but nothing that a chocolate croissant won't cure."

"No, no, no," he argued. "Chocolate soufflé is what you must have. Bertrand, he makes the best in all of Paris."

So soufflé it was, and he was right. It was good, not as good as the conversation, though. We talked nonstop for over an hour. The cool thing was that Etienne didn't just talk about himself. He was sincerely interested in my life. I told him about Maddie, about bird mail, and I even mentioned church a couple of times.

When I mentioned that I hadn't seen the Eiffel Tower up close yet, Etienne acted like a major crime had been committed. "No!" he gasped as he stood up and grabbed his coat. "You must see it. We go now!" With that, he grabbed my hand and led me out the door. The amazing thing is that he didn't let go of my hand during the entire seven-block walk!

Since he was used to all this pop star stuff, Etienne knew exactly where to go to avoid the paparazzi that seemed to constantly stalk us in this country. We followed a tree-lined, cobblestone path along the river, silently watching boats as they glided past and dodging anyone who looked remotely like a photographer. Etienne, my watchful tour guide, seemed to be enjoying the city through my eyes. I mean, Paris was his home. He had reason to be proud. After cutting through a centuries-old neighborhood, we went through the iron gates of a tiny park and up the back slope of a grassy hill.

That's when I saw it, the Eiffel Tower, closer than I'd ever seen it. It was lit up like a Christmas tree and looked even more beautiful than it did in the movies. I'm almost embarrassed to say this, but I cried when I saw it.

He laid his coat down for us to sit on, and we just stared in silence.

"I wish my mom could see this," I thought out loud.

"Maybe she does," he said quietly.

After twenty minutes or so of simply absorbing the view, it was time to go. But the most mind-blowing part of the evening was still to come.

After Etienne helped me up, we found ourselves just staring at each other. That's when it happened. He suddenly swept my bangs to the side, held my face in his hands, and kissed me. And you know what? I kissed back.

By the time we got back to the hotel at around 10:00, I felt amazingly wonderful.

And, well . . . pretty horrible too.

Too tired to figure this all out right now.

More drama on my video blog:
www.izzyspopstarplan.com/videos.
Click on Day 51.

---

4 COMMENTS:

Pastor Ryan said . . .

Okay, I've been trying to let you sort stuff out yourself because you're a big kid now, but I really need to step in and say something here. 1 Timothy 1:19 talks about "holding on to faith and a good conscience." Then it says, "Some have rejected these and so have shipwrecked their faith." Izzy, it's your conscience that's bugging you. You went against your dad's dating rule, and you lied in order to get away with it. Not a good thing, my friend.
Posted Wednesday, 12:25 p.m.

Izzy said . . .

I didn't exactly lie though.
Posted Wednesday, 3:23 p.m.

Pastor Ryan said . . .

Lying isn't always about what you say, Iz. It's sometimes about what you don't say. You gave your dad the *impression* that you were going out with Atsumi. You *led him* to believe something that wasn't true. That's flat-out being dishonest. I'm worried about you, Iz. Please don't shipwreck your faith because of a guy.
Posted Wednesday, 4:26 p.m.

Stephanie said . . .

Lord, please help Izzy sort all this out. Amen.
Posted Wednesday, 4:52 p.m.

Day 52: Oh No!

Mood Meter: Crushed

I cancelled rehearsal today because there is no more music in this devastated heart of mine. I'm pins-in-my-heart hurt, over-the-moon embarrassed, and horrifically angry. I can barely see through my tears to blog right now.

Okay, hold yourself together, Iz, here it goes. I was on my way to breakfast with Atsumi. I wanted to tell her all about how my "undate" took a drastic turn toward "dateville," so we walked outside to see if we could find a quiet café somewhere. We've both gotten pretty good at disguising ourselves, so we weren't worried about the paparazzi bugging us or anything.

We had only walked about a block when I saw them, the Paris tabloids. There, plastered all over the tiny newsstand, was a picture of me, KISSING ETIENNE!

The paparazzi must have been hiding, I don't know, in the bushes or something! The front pages of every single paper seemed to be broadcasting that Etienne and I were in love.

I instantly thought of my dad. He'd been going to the newsstand every day to buy the paper. If he saw me and Etienne on the cover, he would be absolutely devastated.

I began running, full-speed, back to the hotel, thinking that maybe I could somehow keep my dad from going outside, for the next ten years or so! But by the time I got back to our suite, it was too late. There on the little round table by the window was a French newspaper, *Le Monde*. Screaming out from the front page was a picture that would ruin our father-daughter relationship forever.

In total frustration, I picked up the paper and tore the front page to pieces. Then, stifling tears, I walked over to my dad's bedroom door. "Daddy," I cried through the locked door. "Can you open the door? I really need to talk to you." I was bawling so hard by this point that I could barely even speak.

"I can't even . . . I can't even talk to you right now," he answered. He was furious; I could tell. I couldn't blame him. In sixteen years of life, I had never hurt him so badly.

"Daddy, pleeeeease!" I begged as I slid down to the floor in a heap of agony. "Open the door!"

I thought I heard his footsteps, but he never came. He stayed locked up in his room, and I stayed next to the door crying . . . for the next hour or so.

Good Night, God

Sorry, guys, no prayer tonight. I've been blowing it so badly lately that I don't even think God would want to listen.

---

2 COMMENTS:

Ms. Adelina said . . .
"The Lord is gracious and compassionate, slow to anger and rich in love" (Psalm 145:8).
Preciosa, never, NEVER say such a thing! You cannot run so far away from God that He cannot still hear you. You must believe me, Isabella. I have made far more mistakes than you in these seventy-eight years of mine, and God, He still hold me gently in His arms, like a mother do with the baby.
Posted Thursday, 9:43 p.m.

Maddie said . . .
Lord, I wish I could be with my dearest friend as she's hurting, but I can't. Please hold her tightly through the pain. Amen.
Posted Thursday, 10:25 p.m.

Day 53: Betrayed

Mood Meter: Fire Red

Have you ever seen in the cartoons when someone is so mad smoke starts coming out of their ears? Well, the smoke alarms should be going off in my room soon, because I am fire-red furious right now.

By accident, I ran into Renee and Christine in the lobby this morning. While I was still puffy-eyed from a tear-drenched morning, they had the nerve to be smiling like circus clowns.

"Have you seen?" Christine asked excitedly, holding up the newest issue of *Entertainment Weekly*. "You made the cover!"

YOUNG LOVE BLOOMS ON THE *Pop Star* STAGE read the headline, yet another painful reminder that my life was in ruins.

"All goes according to plan!" Renee chimed in.

Then it suddenly became clear. "You both planned this, didn't you? You used me to get some publicity!" I cried, grabbing the magazine from Christine's hands and waving it in her face. "Christine, how could you? I totally trusted you!"

"Calm down, Iz," she answered, as if I were the one who had offended her. "You should be *thanking* us for this!"

"*Thanking* you?" I asked angrily, barely even able to get my words out. "You've totally messed up my life, I can't even sing because I'm so stressed, and my dad has barely spoken to me since yesterday. I'm supposed to be thanking you guys for that?"

"Honey," said Renee, as she put her hands on my shoulders condescendingly, "in a few months you'll be making more money than your father ever will. Let the baby sulk. By the time you hit eighteen, you won't need him anymore."

Her last comment really threw me over the edge. I angrily pulled myself away from Renee and headed out the door for a walk. Let the paparazzi snap away at my tear-stained face, I didn't even care anymore. I needed to get outside and clear my head.

Walking along the Seine, I thought long and hard about my relationship with Etienne. He'd been calling and texting me all day long, but I wasn't ready to call him back yet. I mean, what would I say? I totally had feelings for him, but our whole date was just some huge publicity stunt.

Who knows, maybe he's just panicking because we haven't rehearsed in two days now, which reminds me, Performance Night is tomorrow!!

YIKES!

My Heart

The plans of the righteous are just, but the advice of the wicked is deceitful. (Proverbs 12:5)

Okay, I admit it. As much as I would like to fault Christine and Renee for all of this mess, I'm the one to blame. For the last two months, I've had all these beyond wise people around giving me advice, people like Dad, Anders, Pastor Ryan, and Ms. Adelina. And did I listen? No, I totally blew them off. Instead, I listened to people I barely knew, and what did I get? BURNED.

Good Night, God

Help! Amen.

That's my prayer. What's yours?

L8R

---

3 COMMENTS:

Sabine said . . .
Don't feel so bad, Iz. I didn't see that one coming either. ☹
Posted Friday, 4:32 p.m.

Stephanie said . . .
Hey, we're still here, Izzy. Call me, even if it's in the middle of the night for us. We need to chat.
Posted Friday, 5:17 p.m.

Maddie said . . .
Sour ropes on the way. My mom's sending them tomorrow. That always makes you feel better.
Posted Friday, 6:03 p.m.

Day 54: @Performance Night Paris

Mood Meter: Numb

If this whole date nightmare hadn't happened, I would be writing to you about how tonight's performance was an absolute dream. I mean, it had all the makings of a fairy tale come true. I got to wear a gorgeous, light green, $3,000 Arno Kuivert dress. It was simple but elegant, and it was long, I'm talking drag-on-the-ground long. Then I got to walk the red carpet to the backstage area, cameras flashing the whole time. Oh, and the stage! It faced Champ de Mars Park, right in front of the Eiffel Tower. It was totally decked out in candles and surrounded by these beautiful iron torches.

It was all of my dreams wrapped into one dazzling pop star package.

But the date *did* happen, and I *did* disobey my dad. I *did* lie, and what could have been my fairy-tale ending turned out to be one of the worst days of my life.

Two hours before the show I actually felt pretty focused, you know, like I could put my emotions aside and plow through this like a professional. But then everything began to unravel.

Somebody at *Pop Star Challenge* had the idea, probably Renee, that each of the couples should arrive at the big concert together. So, guess what? I had to face Etienne again.

I had been avoiding him for the last couple of days. I even skipped the sound check rehearsal this morning with the Paris Symphony Orchestra, which must have totally freaked Etienne out. I meant to go, really, but I was so stressed about our relationship that I froze and stayed back at the hotel.

I knew I had to pull myself together by concert time. To mess up our duet together would be cruel, to Etienne and to me. So, when five o'clock hit, I gathered all the confidence I had left and headed down the hall to makeup and wardrobe. It took longer than usual, since Christine wasn't there. Her assistant Javier took good care of me, though. He's the one who picked out the Kuivert.

Straightening my dress, I took a final glance at the mirror and slowly walked to a back exit where our limo was waiting.

Sliding in, I noticed Etienne, tux and all, seated across from me. "How are you feeling?" he asked nervously the moment the chauffer shut the door.

"Fine," I said, trying to avoid conversation at all cost.

"I hear your heart, Izzy. You are *not* fine," he continued, with a concerned look.

I wanted so much to just say something, sorry, anything, but the words wouldn't come.

"Please, I care for you, Izzy," he said. "Just tell me what's wrong, so I make things better for us."

His kind words suddenly triggered a flood of emotion. It was as if all the pain and confusion of the last few days finally found a way out of my heart, and the tears began to flow. I just leaned my head on the window and sobbed as the city lights flew by.

I tried to get a grip before we arrived at the Eiffel Tower, but it was useless. By the time we pulled up to the red carpet leading back-stage, I looked, and felt, like a mess. Christine almost had a heart attack when she saw me backstage and started an emergency makeup repair job while the Paris Symphony Orchestra opened the show.

As she put the final rescuing touches on my hair, a production assistant told us that we were on next.

Etienne looked relieved as I met him at the side of the stage. Atsumi and Miklos had just belted out their final notes, and the crowd was going insane. After the judges rained praises on them, they bowed to the thousands in the audience who were still on their feet, and happily headed off stage. They would be an incredibly tough act to follow.

Atsumi gave me a good luck hug as the lights dimmed and the string section painted the evening air. That was our cue. Etienne offered his arm, and we walked onstage. Looking out at the crowd, I was determined to not let the emotions of the past few days ruin my Pop Star Plan.

Etienne sang first. If our relationship were affecting him at all, he wasn't showing it. He was born to perform and had the audience in the palm of his hands from his first word. Unfortunately, my turn came next. From the second I sang my first note, I knew I was off-key. I tried to fix my pitch mid-sentence, but that only made things worse. I began to panic, and then committed a fatal *Pop Star Challenge* error—I started singing with my head and not my heart.

"And my lonely heart, it feels so warm, and for just this moment we have calmed the storm," I sang like a robot. Oh, the words were all there, and I actually was able to pull it back on key, but the heart and soul that had brought me this far on the show were completely gone.

The orchestra played on through the verse, and I barely survived. Luckily, it was Etienne's turn to sing, and I had a few seconds to regain focus before it was my turn to sing again. I felt like I was able to show a little emotion by the final chorus, but by then it was too late. I had completely ruined my chances of moving on to the next round.

If you think I'm exaggerating, just listen to what Giuseppe Rossi had to say. "I am sorry, but today, you sing your last song on the world stage."

I can almost read the headlines. YOUNG GIRL'S DREAMS DIE TRAGICALLY!

I feel like God wasn't even there tonight, and I don't blame Him. I totally deserve this.

---

4 COMMENTS:

Pastor Ryan said . . .
"He does not treat us as our sins deserve or repay us according to our iniquities. For as high as the heavens are above the earth, so great is his love for those who fear him" (Psalm 103:10–11).
Okay, so you've made a couple of bad choices, but that doesn't mean that God has bailed on you. Are you kidding me? He still loves you, He forgives you, and He's right beside you, like always. God NEVER ditches His kids.
Posted Saturday, 2:10 p.m.

Stephanie said . . .
This isn't the end, Izzy; it's just the beginning of what God has planned for you.
Posted Saturday, 2:21 p.m.

Izzy said . . .
Really?
Posted Saturday, 11:34 p.m.

Stephanie said . . .
Really. I promise.
Lord, more than ever before, Izzy needs to know You love her. Please comfort her. Amen.
Posted Saturday, 11:58 p.m.

D@y 55: Decision Day

Mood Meter: Sorry

Mental overload! Feeling guilty about going on that date when I wasn't supposed to, parental unit still hardly speaking to me, no chance of advancing on *Pop Star Challenge*. Disastrously tragic, don't you think?

All these thoughts spinning in my head kept me awake for most of the night. By 4:00 a.m., I gave up on sleep altogether and just got up. Staring down at the street below, it dawned on me. During this whole time in France, I've been neglecting the two things that really held my head together back home: my songwriting and, more importantly, my relationship with God.

I knew exactly what to do. I grabbed my guitar and headed seventeen stories up, to the roof.

The view of Paris from the rooftop garden was INCREDIBLE! After a few minutes of gazing, I pulled my sweater close, perched myself on an old crate, and started to play. As soon as I started to sing, a new song poured out from my soul, a prayer, an apology to my dearest friend, God.

> *I'm sorry I got this all wrong: we were made to be together.*
> *Been on my own for far too long now; we were made to be together.*
> *Down on my knees trying to get it right, when I hear You calling through this dark, dark night—*
> *We were made, we were made, we were made . . .*
> *Made to be together.*

Sobbing uncontrollably, I had trouble getting the words out. I must have looked like some bed-headed maniac up there on the roof, sniveling through the music, but I didn't care. God and I were talking again, and that's all that mattered.

I stayed up there for three hours, just praying, worshipping, and writing, not one, but TWO new songs. By the time the Paris sun had risen from behind the Eiffel Tower, I had made some important decisions about my dad, about Etienne, and more importantly, about my relationship with God.

As I packed up my guitar and headed downstairs, I still felt pretty miserable about everything, but I also felt determined to do what was right, no matter how I felt.

My Heart

If we confess our sins, he is faithful and just and will forgive us our sins and purify us from all unrighteousness. (1 John 1:9)

When I was a kid, I used to have to get allergy shots. I HATED it! After the doctor was done, my mom would wrap me up in her arms and say, "All done now, little one," and then we would go out for ice cream. It was such a relief to get out of that doctor's office.

That's what I felt like tonight. Out there on the roof, when I asked God for forgiveness, it was as if God were giving me this big hug and saying, "All done now, little one."

Maybe now it's time for ice cream!? I sure could use some.

Good Night, God

Lord, thanks for Your forgiveness. Now help me make things right with all the people I've hurt. Amen.

That's my prayer. What's yours?

L8R

---

3 COMMENTS:

Pastor Ryan said . . .
Amen, Iz! By the way, you're not the only one who's messed up. I've been known to make some pretty big mistakes sometimes.
Posted Sunday, 1:11 p.m.

Stephanie said . . .
Believe me. He speaks the truth!
Posted Sunday, 1:43 p.m.

Pastor Ryan said . . .
Hey, don't rub it in!
Posted Sunday 2:13 p.m.

D⊕y 56: Checklist

Mood Meter: Determined

During my prayer time yesterday, I came up with a list, Izzy Baxter's List of Absolutely Necessary Things to Do. The list, which I wrote in my Pop Star Plan journal, included all the things I needed to do, pronto, if I wanted to get my life back on track. I didn't necessarily *want* to do the things on my list, I just *had* to. Here's how the list, and my day, looked.

1. Finish your song. I started writing a new song yesterday, and I absolutely needed to finish it, TODAY (more about that later). Except for a few problems with the bridge, I was able to wrap it up in under an hour. A new record!

2. Talk to Werner about Friday's Vote Night show. For some lame reason, on this Vote Night show they want us to repeat our Eiffel Tower performances. Probably because the show's an hour long, and they need to fill up the time. Since there is a 99.99% chance that I won't be moving on to the next round, I wanted to make sure that my last performance on *International Pop Star Challenge* was my best. As it stood, Etienne and I were supposed to sing "In Love We Hide" for a second time. There was NO WAY I was ever going to sing that song again.

   I knew Werner always had his breakfast in the hotel restaurant at 9, so I waited on a sofa by the elevators until he came down. When I saw him in the lobby, I dashed to his side and began pleading my case. I asked—no, begged him to allow me to sing a different song, the one I had written that morning. After listening to a rough recording of the song on my MP3 player, he took off the headphones and thought for a while. "Okay," he said with a smile. "Just make sure you remember to sing on key this time."

   Yay! Off to checklist item number three!

3. Talk to Dad. The worst thing about this whole Etienne thing has been my dad's reaction. I have never seen him so mad. I mean, he's talking to me again, about unimportant stuff like the weather, but we need to really *talk* before he heads back to the States in a couple of days for a huge computer network setup for Media World. I don't know, ever since Mom died, he's been

a bit of a mess, and going out with Etienne behind his back has made things worse.

I tried to connect with him, right after my rooftop morning, really! I had this gripping apology speech and everything, but when I got back to the room, he was gone. On top of the note I'd left him when I left the room before breakfast was another note saying that he and Anders had taken the train to Lyon for the day to watch a soccer match. They wouldn't be back until late. BUMMER!

4. Buy a French Bible. This was the easiest thing on my list. There's a bookstore a couple of blocks from the hotel, and with some help from Henrique, this cool-looking worker with dreads, I found what I needed in no time at all.

5. Break up with Etienne. In typical Izzy fashion, I'm saving the hardest thing on my list for tomorrow. After praying things through yesterday, I'm pretty sure that God wants me to totally and completely break things off with Etienne. What's going to make this so difficult is that I reeeeeeally like him. I mean, we get along so well, and he's outrageously cool. I've never met anyone like him, and I probably never will. But hey, the most important relationship in my life is with Jesus, and Etienne doesn't know Him. The tragic fact is, if we don't share faith, there's no way a dating relationship is going to work.

We're going to be taping some scenes for Vote Night at the Louvre museum tomorrow. I'll try to catch him during one of our breaks.

Pray that I'll be strong.

My Heart

But as for me and my household, we will serve the Lord.
(Joshua 24:15)

I'm going to be totally honest with you. It's not gonna *feel* good at all to break things off with Etienne. That's why I'm dreading it so much. I mean, what I really feel like doing is reliving our date again and again and again until the end of time. But faith isn't just about *feelings*; it's about making choices.

So today, however bad it hurts, I'm making a choice to do what God wants. As for Izzy Baxter, I will serve the Lord.

Good Night, God

Lord, please give me the strength to do what's right, even when I don't feel like it. Amen.

That's my prayer. What's yours?

L8R

---

1 COMMENT:

Maddie said . . .

You're my hero, Iz. I'll be praying for you.

Posted Monday, 2:54 p.m.

Day 57: The Louvre

Mood Meter: Rainy-Day Heart

I know what you're all wondering. Yes, I did talk to Etienne today. *Horrifically painful* is what I have to say about that.

The whole day started out pretty yucky, with this huge European storm dumping buckets of rain on everything and everyone in sight. It was almost as if some movie director were setting the scene for the depressing end of my *Pop Star Challenge* romance.

Atsumi sat next to me during the ride to the museum. Good thing, because talking to her kept my mind off of Etienne, at least for the ten minutes it took to get there.

The plan was to film the *Pop Star* gang "happily" strolling through the Louvre, pointing at the *Mona Lisa* and stuff. I'm telling you right now, it was almost IMPOSSIBLE to act happy considering that I was about to lose Etienne and was facing certain doom on Thursday's Vote Night show.

I prayed for the right time to talk to Etienne all day long, but I didn't get a chance until after we wrapped. While the production crew was packing up, I saw him head up these cement stairs. I set my water bottle down and began to follow. By the time I caught up, he was sitting against the wall of this big room staring at a painting of a royal-looking guy with long, curly hair.

"Miklos would kill for hair like that," I said, as I sat down beside him.

"It's King Louis the Fourteenth," he said, smiling nervously, probably wondering why I was suddenly talking to him after ignoring him all week.

"French?" I asked, trying to keep the conversation going.

"Yes, a very special king," he answered patiently. "The painting was supposed to be a gift to the king of Spain, but the French, we love it so much that we take it back."

Now was as good a time as any, so I decided to dive right in. "I have a gift for you," I said, handing him the small brown book I had purchased the day before. "I promise not to take it back."

He smiled and looked at the cover. "It's a Bible."

"In French." I smiled. "It's my favorite book in the whole world. It has the answers to, well, everything."

"Well, that's good, because I've been having a lot of questions." He laughed. "Especially about us."

That was my cue. I began telling him everything, about how I had broken my dad's "no dating until eighteen" policy, about how hard it would be to date someone who didn't share my faith. Most importantly, though, I told him about how much Jesus loved him.

Had he gotten upset, the whole conversation would have been easy. But he didn't, and that made it worse. As I got up to go, I gave him the lyrics to the newest song I had been working on.

"What's this?" he asked dejectedly as he looked over the words.

"It's a song, about us." I said wiping the tears that had begun to flow like a waterfall. "I'm singing it on Thursday."

"Beautiful," he said dejectedly, "like you." With that he got up off the floor and gave me a hug, our last.

As I watched him walk away, I pulled up my scarf. It was going to be a cold night.

My Heart

The LORD is close to the brokenhearted and saves those who are crushed in spirit. (Psalm 34:18)

I'm feeling absolutely crushed tonight. It's one of those nights where I wonder if I'll ever feel happy again. I'm already starting to miss Etienne. I miss my dad, and I TOTALLY miss my mom. I wish I could just lie in her arms and cry, if only for a minute.

But I can lie in God's arms. The Bible says He's "close to the brokenhearted," so even though I'm tragically depressed, I'm not alone. He's here, crying with me. I just need to keep remembering that, and I think I'll be okay. I mean, isn't that what faith is all about?

Good Night, God

Lord, I'm hurting. Please let me know You're near. Amen.
That's my prayer. What's yours?
L8R

3 COMMENTS:

Pastor Ryan said . . .

Remember, Iz, you are *not* alone. We had a special prayer meeting
tonight, just for you! Twenty-seven of your truest friends were down
on their knees asking God to help you through. You're gonna make it.
Posted Tuesday, 10:09 p.m.

Stephanie said . . .

Hang in there, Izzy. You don't know what God has planned. Just wait, my
friend.
Posted Tuesday, 10:23 p.m.

Maddie said . . .

If it makes you feel any better, LuLu's is naming a smoothie after its most
famous customer: *Izzy Berry Delight*. Hope to hear your wonderfully
loud laugh again, Iz. ☺
Posted Tuesday, 11:09 p.m.

Day 58: Rush!

Mood Meter: Out of Breath

I got home extremely late last night. I guess they needed more tape of us pop stars "having fun" because after our little trip to the Louvre, they took us to dinner at this fancy restaurant. After eating a meal of escargot and lamb (yuck!), we got a surprise visit from none other than Tony Delarussa, a famous singer from the forties. He gave us some advice on being famous and stuff, none of which I really listened to because I was DYING to get back to the hotel. There was still one item on my to-do list, talk to Dad. His flight was leaving early the next morning, so I absolutely had to catch him before he went to bed!

When I finally got back to our hotel suite, everything was quiet. Anders was asleep on the pull-out sofa with the TV on, as usual, and my dad was snoring away in his bedroom. I was too late. After debating whether I should wake him up or not, I reluctantly decided to let him sleep. I figured I could just get up early and talk to him before he left. EPIC MISTAKE!

Waking up the next morning, I noticed an envelope on my pillow. The "Izzy" on the front was in my dad's printing. Before I could open it, I noticed the time, seven. Suddenly, a sickening fact dawned on me; I had overslept, BY ALMOST AN HOUR!

I frantically shoved the envelope in my pocket, pulled on my sweatshirt, and raced, slippers on, downstairs. Panting, I desperately begged the concierge to find a driver to take me to the airport. With none available, she offered to drive me herself.

Near tears, I ran to her small BMW and we shot off toward Charles de Gaulle. During the thirty minutes it took to get there, I ripped open my dad's letter and began to read.

My Dearest Izzy,

I wanted to talk to you before I left, but I didn't have the heart to wake you. Just know that I'm so sorry for the way I've been acting lately. I'm not the greatest with words, like Mom was, and I freeze up when I can't find the right thing to say. There's one thing I do know how to say, though. I

love you, and there is nothing you could ever do to take that away.
Love,
Dad

Reading his words made me even more determined. I had to find him, no matter how crowded the airport was.

As we pulled up to the Air France terminal, I said bye to my driver and dashed off. Weaving my way through countless lines of luggage-toting tourists, I searched madly for my dad and the forgiveness I so desperately needed. After twenty minutes of hopeless searching, I looked up at the departure sign. My dad's flight was already board-ing. I sank down against a luggage cart and practically pulled my hair out in desperation. I had missed my chance to make things right.

Just then I noticed a man at the front of a long security line. He was wearing the same jeans and khaki jacket my dad usually wore. I stood up to get a better view of the guy, who was now putting his hand luggage on an x-ray machine's conveyor belt. Could it be him? I wondered. It was!

"Daddy!" I yelled at the top of my lungs. He turned around at the sound of my voice. Leaving the line, and his luggage, he began to run toward me. I ran into his arms and gave him the tightest hug ever.

"I'm so, so sorry," I bawled. "I've been a total loser. I'll never lie to you again."

"You're not a loser," he said, through a couple of tears of his own. "You're my daughter."

By now, we had drawn the attention of a throng of onlookers, not to mention several paparazzi. We must have looked like a frazzled mess of tears and hugs, but I didn't care. We headed over to a couple of seats and just talked for hours, about my date, my Performance Night mess-up, and, of course, Mom. My dad ended up missing his flight, but he didn't care. We were okay now, and that's all that really mattered.

Luckily, he was able to book a later flight. I would never be able to live with myself had he missed his meeting on Thursday.

When it was time to leave, my dad pulled me an arm's length away, wiped my tears away, and said the words I had longed to hear all week.

"All done now, little one."

My Heart

But while he was still a long way off, his father saw him and was filled with compassion for him; he ran to his son, threw his arms around him and kissed him. (Luke 15:20)

The story of the prodigal son has become my new all-time favorite in the Bible. It's about a son who totally messed up his life. When he came back to his father, his father totally forgave him and threw a big party for him. Jesus told this story to show what God does when we are sorry for the messes we've made. Instead of punishing us, He runs up to us and gives us this huge hug. It's a great story. You should check it out.

Good Night, God

Lord, thanks for running to me instead of away. Amen.
That's my prayer. What's yours?
L8R

---

2 COMMENTS:

James Baxter said . . .
Okay, I'm on the plane right now reading your blogs, and I feel like an idiot. I can't believe I've been missing all this drama in your life! I can't even begin to tell you how sorry I am.
Posted Wednesday, 9:32 p.m.

Izzy said . . .
No worries. All over now. Sleep tight, Daddy.
Posted Wednesday, 10:43 p.m.

Day 59: @Vote Night Paris

Mood Meter: You'll See

If my life was a ride, it would definitely be the huge monster coaster at Holiday Island, you know, the one with the three loops and the 140-foot drop. Today was definitely wild.

Vote Night was at the Paris Opera House this time around, the largest opera house in the world. I didn't want a repeat of my Eiffel Tower nightmare, so I arrived early to work on my song for the night. I was the first contestant there, and I got the place to myself for a while. Staring at the ornate balconies, I wondered if Ms. Adelina had ever performed here.

Eventually, the rest of the *Pop Star* gang started to trickle in, and the whole night started to feel a bit awkward. I mean, the other contestants knew that I would be one of the ones going home tonight. So they just avoided contact with me altogether, probably because they didn't know what to say. Atsumi tried to be encouraging, but it wasn't working. I mean, I knew the truth as well as everyone else.

Overall, it was a pretty average Vote Night with the usual video clips, repeat performances, and judge's comments. But then came my turn, and average was not an option.

Thanks to Renee, my whole mess had gone public—the date with Etienne, going against my father's wishes, everything. The tabloids had gotten it all wrong, though, and tonight I wanted my performance to set the record straight.

I picked up my guitar like a warrior and headed toward my moment of truth. On the way, I heard someone call from behind. It was Miklos. "Izzy," he shouted as I turned to look. "America, rock and roll!" I flashed him a thankful smile and headed onstage.

A hush fell upon the audience as I stepped into the spotlight and the piano began its intro. They knew this would be my last performance. I took a deep breath and hit my opening chord. Then I let my newest song pour out of me like tears.

If we don't have faith, we don't have enough.
Though my heart is weak, and my soul grows tired,
I can't fall in love
If we don't have faith.

Usually I would have been ultra paranoid about every move, about every note I sang on that stage. But not tonight. Tonight, I felt like I was on the fire escape back home. It was just me, singing my story.

Oh yeah, I'm sure you want to hear who's going on, so here it goes.

Who's going to Argentina?

Edina Hayner, Etienne Rousseau, Atsumi Takenaga, Miklos Szabo, and, drum roll please . . .

IZZY BAXTER!!!!!!

My Heart

For it is by grace you have been saved, through faith—and this not from yourselves, it is the gift of God. (Ephesians 2:8)

Grace = being given kindness and favor when we totally don't deserve it.

I totally don't deserve to make it through to the next round. Seriously, I totally messed up my song, I broke my dad's dating rule, and, on top of that, I lied about it. Face it; I should be heading back to L.A. But I'm not, and that's because of a little thing called grace.

The sweetest thing about God is that He is full of grace. I mean, He's always pouring gifts on us that we *don't* deserve. He gave His only Son to die on the cross for us while we were still sinners! That is just crazy cool.

Good Night, God

God, Your amazing grace rocks! Amen.
That's my prayer. What's yours?
L8R

3 COMMENTS:

James Baxter said . . .
I actually made it home in time for the show! Amazing!
Posted Thursday, 11:01 p.m.

Pastor Ryan said . . .
Izzy's back in town!
Posted Thursday, 11:03 p.m.

Sabine said . . .
Seriouslyawesomeandwonderfully EPIC performance!
Posted Thursday, 11:07 p.m.

D⊕y 60: Air Traffic Streams

Mood Meter: Over-the-Sea Smile

I'm blogging from high above the ocean blue! According to the little TV map thing in front of my seat, we've just left European airspace. Good-bye, France. Argentina, here I come!

I'm actually glad to be leaving Paris since my time there pretty much stunk, big time. Okay, to be fair, I did have a couple of good days, like today. Today was pretty awesome.

At around two, a shuttle bus took the five remaining contestants and some of the crew to CDG—that's what we frequent fliers call the Paris airport (ha ha). Anders, my official babysitter and manager, had headed to the airport earlier in the day to check in our bags and work out some last-minute details. I kind of wish he had been on the shuttle with me because I had said some pretty awful things to him, and I wanted to make sure we were okay.

When we arrived at our terminal, I headed directly to the VIP lounge to see if I could find him. "Yes!" I whispered to myself as I spied him sitting on a sofa next to this floor-to-ceiling window. I plopped myself down next to him and, without a word, gave him a hug.

"What was that for?" He smiled.

"I'm so sorry," I said, as the tears began to roll. "You were giving me awesome advice. I just didn't want to listen."

"It's okay, Iz," he said, "really."

"No, it's not," I persisted. "I said some pretty mean things."

Anders has always been an awesome listener, and I could tell my words were hitting home. "I'm sorry for saying that you're wasting your life in front of a laptop," I cried. "You're gonna do great things in your life, Anders. I know it."

"You don't have to apologize," he said. "I've been thinking about what you said. You were right."

"NO!" I practically screamed. "I wasn't right. I was wrong, totally wrong."

"Izzy," he said, "I've been hiding behind my schoolbooks for years. Relationships, though, they scare me. I don't do them well at all."

"Please don't say that, Anders," I pleaded with him, thinking that his sudden revelation was all my fault.

"It's okay, Iz." He smiled as he gave me a hug. "I'm trying to change. Today, I asked Atsumi if she wanted to sit by me on the plane."

"And?" I gasped, pushing him arm's length away so that I could see his expression.

"And she said yes."

Okay, at this point I practically knocked him over with my screams of happiness. I couldn't believe it. My brother was finally deciding to share his heart with someone.

About an hour later, when they finally called for our flight to board, I looked up and saw something crazy beautiful. Anders was walking up the tunnel, holding Atsumi's bag for her. The two were beaming as they chatted away like lifelong friends.

Following from a distance, I couldn't help but smile, and deep within I could hear a soul song rising.

Vive l'amour!

Long live love!

My Heart

And now these three remain: faith, hope and love. But the greatest of these is love. (1 Corinthians 13:13)

I know I've made it sound like dating is a total nightmare, but it really doesn't have to be. When it's the right time, when you're old enough, and it's the right person, dating can turn into love, and love is beautiful. I mean, God wants us to find love. He invented it. Okay, I may be a bit young for it now, but one day, when the time is right, God is going to bring me someone I can love forever. Until then I'll pray that I can be the right person for him. I can't wait.

Good Night, God

Lord, when the right guy comes along, help me do this whole dating thing right. It's too important to mess up. Amen.

That's my prayer. What's yours?

L8R

---

1 COMMENT:

James Baxter said . . .
It's about time that boy found a friend! ☺
Posted Friday, 10:32 p.m.

PART 4

Good-bye, Buenos Aires

Can you lift me up
High above these waters?
Can you lift me up
Higher than these fears?

"SING"—IZZY BAXTER

D@y 61: Turbulence

Mood Meter: Rolling with the Airwaves

We were flying for most of the day today, or should I say bouncing. TURBULENCE! There was this major thunderstorm over the Atlantic, so the captain kept us in our seats for five hours of the flight. Not fun.

Christine was sitting across the aisle a couple of rows back. She had a death grip on the armrests, and her eyes were as big as DVDs. I was still pretty upset at Renee and her for tipping off the Paris tabloids about my date, but seeing the fear in her eyes made me feel kind of sorry for her.

I'd already forgiven Christine in my prayers, but forgiveness is more than a prayer; it's a verb. Living on the wild side, I unbuckled my seatbelt and dashed to the empty seat next to her.

"Isn't it amazing?" I said, as I buckled myself in. "The wings of a Boeing 777 can bend nearly ninety degrees without breaking off."

"So you're a pop star *and* an aeronautical engineer?" she answered, with a nervous smile.

"It's my brother's fault." I laughed. "He knows everything about everything."

"So you're not scared?" she asked, her voice quivering.

"Not really," I replied, hoping my calm tone of voice would help her relax.

"Izzy," she asked after a long pause. "How come you always seem so . . . so brave?"

"Oh, trust me," I retorted. "I'm the biggest wimp there is. I still sleep with the light on sometimes."

"I'm not buying it," she continued. "Look, you broke off your relationship with the coolest star on the planet, and then you went and sang your own song even though you knew it could cost you popularity points. That took a lot of courage. I could never go against the flow like that."

Realizing that this was an open door to tell her about God, I said a quick prayer before answering. "Well, I guess I just know that if I do the right thing, God is going to take care of me, no matter what happens."

We ended up talking about God for a while, and she was actually listening. When the flight attendants began rolling the breakfast cart down the aisle, it was time to go back to my seat. "He's here with us right now, Christine," I assured her. "We're gonna get to Buenos Aires in one piece."

"Izzy," she said, "I feel horrible about the whole tabloid thing. I'm totally, totally sorry. I tend to just follow along with whatever Renee says sometimes."

"And I totally, totally forgive you," I said, as the captain turned off the seatbelt sign.

With a smile in my heart, I headed back to my seat for some breakfast. The rest of the flight would be smooth sailing.

My Heart

Then Peter came to Jesus and asked, "Lord, how many times shall I forgive my brother when he sins against me? Up to seven times?" Jesus answered, "I tell you, not seven times, but seventy-seven times." (Matthew 18:21–22)

It felt so good to say those three words today, "I forgive you." It wouldn't have done me an ounce of good to hold on to my anger. Bitterness just eats us up inside because we were born to let go, born to forgive, born to love.

Good Night, God

Lord, help me forgive others just like You have forgiven me. Amen. That's my prayer. What's yours?
L8R

---

1 COMMENT:

Stephanie said . . .
Amen! Grace and forgiveness are the glue that keeps relationships together. Without them, we wouldn't have any friendships at all.
Posted Saturday, 1:04 p.m.

D@y 62: Anonymous

Mood Meter: Viva Argentina!

We arrived in Argentina early this morning. I was tired, but too excited to sleep. We were in an entirely different continent, and I just wanted to drink it all in!

Buenos Aires looked beautiful from the window of our airport shuttle bus, and I couldn't wait to explore. After dropping off our luggage at the Rey de Recoleta Hotel, I asked Anders and Atsumi if they wanted to check out the neighborhood. I guess they had enjoyed hanging together on the flight over, because they both jumped at the chance.

Strolling along tree-lined streets, we basked in the early morning sunlight. The seasons are opposite here in South America, so when it's fall in Europe, it's spring here! While Anders and Atsumi excitedly discussed the old French architecture they were seeing, I stared as elegantly dressed ladies walked tiny poodles and gray-haired men sipped Argentine tea in sidewalk cafés.

The coolest thing about Argentina so far is that I can be pretty anonymous over here. Argentine contestant Carlos Pereira was knocked out in the first round, and the entire nation had stopped caring about the show ever since. Gone are the photo-starved paparazzi and tabloid headlines. But I'm still kind of paranoid. There's bound to be some French photographers hiding out there somewhere, just dying to get a shot of me and Etienne talking to each other. That's *not* going to happen, at least not for a while. It's really awkward between us now, so we've both been kind of avoiding each other.

We had a light lunch at *La Biela*, this overpriced café, and then headed back to our hotel for an afternoon nap. Unfortunately, what I found in my room kept me from catching the nap I needed. There, in the center of the room, was this huge box. At first I thought it was some kind of gift from the studio or something, but then I saw my dad's writing and realized exactly what it was, MY TEXTBOOKS! All of my morning joy instantly disappeared.

In all of the pop star madness of the last several weeks, I had entirely forgotten. School was starting in a week.

Noooooooo!

My Heart

Sow your seed in the morning, and at evening let not your hands be idle, for you do not know which will succeed, whether this or that, or whether both will do equally well. (Ecclesiastes 11:6)

Okay, there's something you all need to know about me. I don't like school. Don't get me wrong, I'm good at school, and I get good grades. It's just that listening to lectures online and staring at school books can be so boring. I'm an artist. I want to play music, write songs, and perform. That's what inspires me, gives me energy. I just want to spend my days singing.

But school is what God has put on my plate right now, and I need to do it the best I can. I don't know exactly what job I'll end up having, or where my life will end up right now, so I need to work hard at my music *and* work just as hard at school.

Good Night, God

Help me do the boring but necessary things in life well, Lord, even if they don't thrill me. Amen.
That's my prayer. What's yours?
L8R

---

1 COMMENT:

Anders said . . .
I've got something I need to tell you.
Posted Sunday 8:34 p.m.

Day 63: @Challenge Night Buenos Aires

Mood Meter: Getting Worried

Challenge Night was kind of low-key tonight. Since there were only five performers left, there wasn't an opening number to perform, and we didn't have to dress up or anything. Because of that, Atsumi, Miklos, Edina, and I were able to spend our hours before showtime playing a relaxed game of Monopoly backstage. By the time Sean Moore opened the show, we were mellow like a summer morning.

Etienne, on the other hand, kept pretty much to himself. That's not like him. In fact, he's been looking pretty depressed lately. I'm kind of worried about him.

We taped in this hundred-year-old tango club, which was a pretty small venue for us. The audience wrapped around the stage like a horseshoe, and we sat on stools in the middle as they showed clips of our journey through the show. As the screen flashed back to my first audition, I barely recognized the insecure little girl stumbling through "How Can I Keep from Singing." Seriously, I've changed so much since the show started that I don't even know who I am anymore. That, my friends, frightens me.

After a high-speed video collage of our airport encounters over the show, the three judges stepped onto the small stage. Then Aiko Mae, as elegant as ever, dramatically opened the envelope to reveal our next challenge.

"*International Pop Star Challenge* contestants," she said solemnly. "in the past months you have experienced what it is like to be famous. You have appeared live onstage and on television, and you have moved the hearts of millions."

"Yes, many fans, they find you," continued Giuseppe Rossi, "but maybe fame causes you to lose yourself."

"In your journey as an artist, you must strive to avoid this," said a fatherly looking Marshall Phillips. "This week we challenge you to find yourself again. Once you have, we'd like you to share who you are with the world, right here on the *International Pop Star Challenge* stage."

After some closing words by Sean Moore, the theme music came on, and it was a wrap.

Stepping offstage, I got a call from my dad. Since the show doesn't come on until prime time in the U.S., he wanted to know how everything went, so I gave him the scoop.

Before we hung up, I asked him if he had seen Ms. Adelina. I hadn't heard from her in over a week, no calls, e-mails, blog comments, nothing, so I was starting to worry. He said he was worried too, because earlier in the day he had gone over to her apartment to show her some pictures from Japan, and she didn't answer.

He promised to check with the landlord and neighbors in the morning, but that's not making me feel any better.

Ms. Adelina, where are you?

My Heart

God is within her, she will not fall; God will help her at break of day. (Psalm 46:5)

I have a choice now. I can stay awake all night worrying about Ms. Adelina, or I can just pray and give the whole thing over to God. I'm going to try the trusting God route. There's nothing else I can do. Jesus has Ms. Adelina in His arms. She belongs to Him, and wherever she is, He's gonna take care of her.

Good Night, God

Lord, help me trust that You'll take care of the ones I love. Amen.

That's my prayer. What's yours?

L8R

---

1 COMMENT:

Maddie said . . .
We've been worried about her too. She hasn't been singing at night lately. Pretty strange, huh?
Posted Monday, 7:07 p.m.

Day 64: Alone

Mood Meter: Sadly Joyful

There are different types of good news. There's the kind of good news that makes a person just plain happy, like "You just won a million dollars!" and then there's the kind of news that makes a person happy but tragically sad at the same time, like the news that Anders dropped on me today.

He kept telling me he wanted to talk to me, but with Challenge Night and all, we never found time to connect. So this morning I made it a point to catch him before heading to the studio to go over song choices for Performance Night.

When I caught up with him, he was researching past *International Pop Star Challenge* winners and trying to calculate what types of songs earned the most votes. I don't think he was getting very far, because when I asked him if he wanted to go for a walk, he looked relieved. We headed down Avenida Santa Fe to this ice cream shop called La Veneciana that everyone around here was raving about.

Finding the last two seats in the place, I cut straight to the chase. "So what's this *important news* you're dying to tell me?"

With a huge grin on his face, he pulled a folded letter from his back pocket, placed it in front of me, and motioned for me to read. "It's from Stanford," he beamed.

"We have looked over your academic record and are proud to say . . ." Without even finishing, I dropped the letter on the table and squealed. "Oh my gosh! You got in!" I yelled, nearly knocking over the table as I reached over to give him a hug. Stanford has been my brother's dream from, like, the day he was born. Getting in was as big to him as getting on *International Pop Star Challenge* was to me. "So when are you going?" I asked.

"Well, this is a last-round admission letter," he answered as our ice cream arrived. "You know, a last-minute acceptance. I'm leaving in four days to go back to Los Angeles and get everything packed."

Realizing what this meant, I dropped my banana-cream-filled spoon back into my bowl. "You mean, you're leaving me here, alone?"

"I worked it all out with Dad. Atsumi's Mom will make sure you're okay," he said, trying to calm the panic that he must have seen rising in my eyes. "You can even stay in their room if you want."

I felt the tears rising, but I pushed them back. I didn't want to ruin his happy moment. I faked a few smiles as I listened to him go on and on about Stanford's awesome engineering program and about the dorms.

When I got back to the hotel room, I locked myself in the bathroom and let it all out. My brother, my dearest friend, was leaving, not only Buenos Aires, but home.

This is going to hurt.

My Heart

When I was a child, I talked like a child, I thought like a child, I reasoned like a child. When I became a man, I put childish ways behind me. (1 Corinthians 13:11)

My dad is gone, Ms. Adelina has disappeared, and now my brother is leaving. Is this some kind of initiation into the world of adulthood or something? It's scary. I've always relied on my dad and brother when it comes to my spiritual life. I still do. That's worked fine, but I'm older now and starting to realize that there are gonna be times in life when God's the only One listening. I need to be able to trust in Him during those times.

Good Night, God

Lord, as I grow older, the world is getting more complicated. Please help me make it through. Amen.

That's my prayer. What's yours?

L8R

---

1 COMMENT:

Stephanie said . . .
Life gets more complicated, but it also gets more beautiful. Just wait.
You'll see.
Posted Tuesday, 8:02 p.m.

D@y 65: Cry

Mood Meter: Making Miserable Lists

Grade for the day: F–

The whole sorry parade started at around noon when my dad called with awful news about Ms. Adelina. He had gone door-to-door asking neighbors if they had seen her lately, and none had. It's been almost two weeks since she's come out to sing, and they're all worried. A million questions are spinning through my head right now. Is she sick? Did she move without telling us? My dad said he would get back to me as soon as he got some more info, so I've been glued to my cell all day.

Now, you have to know this about me. I have this horrible habit. When I hear tragically bad news, I start thinking about all the other terrible things going on in my life. One thing leads to another, and pretty soon I'm caught up in this mega wave of woe. Brace yourself, here it comes.

Another person in my life who's gone missing is ME, to Maddie, that is. I've been so wrapped up in my pop star life that I've totally disappeared as a friend. I haven't been texting, calling, anything. I can't believe what a total loser I've been. Here I am telling her that she can design my dresses and stuff, and then I just totally ditch her. She still comments on my blog, but I know that she's probably hurt. I feel like walking over to her apartment and just begging for forgiveness. But, of course, I can't. I'm five thousand miles away, in a different world. Maddie, if you're reading this, SORRY FOR BEING SUCH A LOUSY FRIEND!

The last thing on my list of woeful things is Etienne. I miss him, A LOT. I wish we could just hang out and talk like we did before the whole date mess. He's been totally miserable, I can tell. The worst thing about it is that it's been affecting his music. I heard him at the practice studio today, and he sounded pretty distracted. Luke, the show's ultra mellow keyboard player, was actually getting pretty frustrated with him. If only I were two years older and he were a Christian, then we could ride off into the sunset in a fairy-tale ending. Like that's ever going to happen.

Anyway, I'm miserablymournfullikearainyday.

My Heart

I have told you these things, so that in me you may have peace. In this world you will have trouble. But take heart! I have overcome the world. (John 16:33)

Sometimes I feel like all the bad things happening in my life are all my fault, like it's God's punishment for all the times I've messed up lately. Deep down, I know that's not true though. God's forgiven me, 100 percent. It's just that I have a hard time accepting that forgiveness.

We're all gonna go through hard times in our lives sometimes. That's the way life is. We just need to remember that God isn't against us during those times. He's on our side, and He's gonna guide us through the pain.

Good Night, God

I know You love me, Lord, but I don't feel it. Can You please remind me? Amen.

That's my prayer. What's yours?

L8R

---

1 COMMENT:

James Baxter said . . .
Izzy, I just thought of something. Call me when you wake up.
Posted Wednesday, 11:32 p.m.

D@y 66: Te Amo

Mood Meter: Grateful

I'm feeling better today. For one thing, I got to talk to Daddy, two days in a row now. He called me this morning, bright and early. He had good news, well, kind of.

"Didn't Ms. Adelina say something about still having a brother in Argentina?" he shouted through a bad connection.

"Yeah, in San Telmo," I answered. "But who in the world knows where that is?"

"It's in Buenos Aires, Izzy, about a mile from where you are!" he answered excitedly.

"What?" I said, still puzzled.

"San Telmo is a neighborhood in Buenos Aires. Find Ms. Adelina's brother, and you just might be able to find Ms. Adelina."

I thanked my dad, hung up the phone, and raced across the street to a coffee shop where Anders was hanging out with Atsumi. After explaining the situation, I hurried to San Telmo with the two lovebirds joining me.

San Telmo, the oldest neighborhood in the city, was packed with people. As we made our way along cobblestone streets, past groups of artists and street musicians, we asked everyone in sight if they knew of Adelina Farinelli, the opera singer. Finding someone who spoke English was hard; finding someone who'd even heard of Ms. Adelina was even harder.

We searched until way past lunch, and when our feet could take no more, we crashed, streetside, at an outdoor café. I was feeling pretty discouraged at the hopelessness of the situation, when a band of street musicians set up and started playing next to us.

"Te amo, te amo, te amo," they sang repeatedly, strumming away on their guitars. Recognizing us, they called us over to sing with them. Atsumi and I had no idea what we were singing, but we were totally getting into it. It felt good to just dance our worries away there on those ancient streets. Eventually, the lead singer slowed the music down and sang these beautiful-sounding lines.

> *No importa donde, no importa cuando.*
> *Sin pregunta, y para siempre*
> *Te amo.*

"That sounds beautiful," I told the teenage-looking guy when he was finished. "What does it mean?"

"It an old song," he said in faltering English. "It say:

> *"It doesn't matter where. It doesn't matter when.*
> *Without question, and forever*
> *I will always love you."*

I loved the lyrics so much, I asked him to write them down for me, and he did. As I watched him write them down on a napkin, I remembered last night's prayer. I had asked for God to show me His love, and through the song of some street musicians, He had.

My Heart

Then a great and powerful wind tore the mountains apart and shattered the rocks before the LORD, *but the* LORD *was not in the wind. After the wind there was an earthquake, but the* LORD *was not in the earthquake. After the earthquake came a fire, but the* LORD *was not in the fire. And after the fire came a gentle whisper.* (1 Kings 19:11–12)

God talks to us. He really does. He speaks to us from the Bible, He speaks to us through other people, and He speaks to us in gentle whispers that only our hearts can hear.

I want to be listening. Don't you?

Good Night, God

Lord, help us drown out life's noises so that we can hear Your still, small voice. Amen.

That's my prayer. What's yours?

Adios!

---

1 COMMENT:

Pastor Ryan said . . .
Amazing! Can I use your story at group on Monday?
Posted Thursday, 5:22 p.m.

Day 67: Violeta

Mood Meter: More Than Amazed

I woke up with sore feet and an even sorer heart. Sitting up in bed, I wondered if I would ever see Ms. Adelina again. Searching for her brother, Marcelo, in a city of nearly three million people seemed utterly hopeless, and we had run out of options. So I did what I usually do when I'm stressed. I picked up my guitar and headed for the balcony.

I figured, with Performance Night right around the corner, a little rehearsal would do me some good. Seriously now, I don't think any of us want to see a repeat of my Paris performance. Reaching into my guitar case, I saw an old friend, my Pop Star Plan journal. I smiled as I picked it up and flipped through the pages. I couldn't help but laugh as I read some of my earliest rules. Boy, have I changed.

Then I saw it, Pop Star Plan Rule #100: "Never give up." The words jumped off the page and into my heart. "I'm not giving up," I said to myself. "I'm going to find Ms. Adelina no matter what." Ten minutes later Anders and I were back on the street, San Telmo bound.

On our way there, we decided to try a different strategy. We could narrow our search by only talking to people over seventy. They would be more likely to have heard of Ms. Adelina, the opera singer, than someone who was younger.

Allow me to brag a little. Our plan was BRILLIANT. In less than fifteen minutes, we hit the jackpot. The very first person we talked to was this old guy playing chess in the park. He put on his glasses and took a look at the cell phone picture. "Adelina Farinelli," he said matter-of-factly.

"Hermano . . . brother?" asked Anders using the minimal amount of Spanish he knew.

"*Sí, sí,*" answered the gentleman, smiling to show he understood. Then he said something in Spanish to the man sitting across from him on the bench, and the two started laughing.

With that, his chess partner took off his hat and introduced himself in fluent English. "Marcelo. My name is Marcelo Farinelli."

If that's not a God thing, I don't know what is. This random man we had found on a park bench was Ms. Adelina's brother! I immediately began pelting him with questions, desperate to find out about my dear friend. But Marcelo wouldn't answer. "No, no, no," he scolded, finger raised. "First, we have tea." With that, we impatiently followed him across the street to his apartment, where he poured us a gourd full of Argentine tea.

"Now, we talk," he said, pulling out an old album that overflowed with newspaper clippings and photographs. We spent over an hour pouring over black-and-white photos of Ms. Adelina singing as a child, and, later in life, performing at some of the great opera houses of the world.

I could see tears forming at the edge of Marcelo's eyes as he stared at a picture of himself playing an accordion, while a teenage Ms. Adelina sang to a small crowd. "We have a singing group. We play all over Buenos Aires," he said softly. "This is the last time we play."

"Why?" I asked.

"She move to Los Angeles even though my father tell her stay, but she go anyway. After two years her singing not go so well, and she too embarrassed to come home. Now we both not have the money to visit," he answered with a sigh. "But still, we write letters, and now the e-mails."

"Do you know where she is?" I stepped in. "We haven't heard from her in many days."

"She send me an e-mail a few weeks ago," he said, wiping his eyes as he answered. "She say sorry, sorry for everything, and that maybe one day we sing again."

My heart sank. Marcelo had no idea where his sister was, and we were back to square one. We thanked him for his hospitality and headed for the door. Before we left, he hugged us both and handed me an old sheet of stationery. Though the handwritten words were in Spanish, I recognized the song instantly: "Violeta," Ms. Adelina's nightly musical gift to the neighborhood, a piece she had written herself.

My Heart

What do you think? If a man owns a hundred sheep, and one of them wanders away, will he not leave the ninety-nine on the hills and go to look for the one that wandered off? (Matthew 18:12)

When I was walking through San Telmo today, I thought of this verse. When I was searching for Marcelo, nothing else really mattered. All I wanted to do was find him. It's the same with God. When we're lost, He hunts high and low for us, not relaxing until we're safe in His arms.

Good Night, God

Lord, thanks for finding me. Please help me find Ms. Adelina. Amen.

That's my prayer. What's yours?

Adios!

---

2 COMMENTS:

James Baxter said . . .

I hope you got all his info. We'll have to contact him once we find out where his sister is.

Posted Friday, 6:11 p.m.

Izzy said . . .

Yup, e-mail, phone. I wanted to make sure we could find him again if we had to.

Posted Friday, 11:34 p.m.

Day 68: Good-bye

Mood Meter: Lost and Lonely

My dad finally got word of Ms. Adelina, and it's not good. She's at the UCLA Medical Center, in a coma. A couple of weeks ago the paramedics came to our building at, like, three in the morning and took her away. My dad called the hospital this morning, and they told him that she might not make it through the week.

If that wasn't tragic enough, today is also the day that Anders goes back to Los Angeles. He's going home to get his stuff together before heading to Stanford. After helping him pack, Atsumi and I had lunch with him. I was so stressed about everything that I couldn't even touch my food. I just sat there as Anders kept telling us that we could chat online and stuff. Walking back to the hotel, I felt like just ditching everything and heading home with Anders so I could see Ms. Adelina, but that would mean leaving *International Pop Star Challenge*, and I wasn't sure if I should give up on my dreams.

An hour later the airport shuttle pulled up to the hotel, and it was time for Anders to go. I gave my brother the tightest hug ever, and he hugged me back even tighter. "You're gonna be okay, little sis," he said.

"No, I'm not," I answered, barely holding it together.

After our good-byes, Anders stepped into the van, and I bolted upstairs for a good cry. Getting back to my room, I was hit with an overwhelming wave of sadness. Then, while staring at the empty room, I made a life-changing decision. Leaving over five thousand dollars of borrowed clothes and my *International Pop Star Challenge* dreams behind, I picked up my guitar case and ran downstairs, toward Anders, toward Ms. Adelina.

Anders was still on the curb, talking to Atsumi through an open window, when I burst out of the revolving hotel doors. "Where are you going?" he said with his jaw practically dropping to the curb.

Throwing my guitar case into the luggage compartment, I answered, "With you, of course. Call Dad."

Anders just laughed and said, "Whatever you say, Miss Pop Star."

I guess he's used to the off-the-wall ways of Izzy Baxter.

My Heart

Whoever serves me must follow me; and where I am, my servant also will be. My Father will honor the one who serves me.
(John 12:26)

Today I had to give up a dream, at least for now. Being by Ms. Adelina's side is the right thing to do. It just is. Sure, that stings. But, hey, following God isn't always pain free. Sometimes we have to make sacrifices to do what's right. It isn't always easy, but it's always best. In the end, God honors those who follow Him, and that's a reward you don't want to miss.

Good Night, God

Lord, help me follow You, always. Amen.
That's my prayer. What's yours?
Adios!

---

2 COMMENTS:

Stephanie said . . .
We support you 100 percent. Call me when you get to L.A.
Posted Saturday, 8:17 p.m.

Pastor Ryan said . . .
Don't doubt your decision, no matter what people say. You have to do what you feel God is telling you to do.
Posted Saturday, 11:34 p.m.

Day 69: Pray, Love, Worship

Mood Meter: Dazed

My dad was happy to see me get into the car at LAX today, a little bit worried about my leaving the show, I could tell, but proud. He totally understood why I came back, and drove me straight to the hospital.

It was hard seeing Ms. Adelina at first. She looked so frail lying motionless in her hospital bed, tubes attached to her arms and nose. Each beep of the heart monitor reminded me of my mom's last days at this same place. Pulling up a chair, my dad and I gently grabbed her hands and began to pray.

That's when my cell phone rang. It was *Pop Star Challenge* director Werner, wondering why I didn't show up for rehearsals this morning. Taking a deep breath, I headed for the hallway, dreading the conversation I was about to have.

When I told him I was in Los Angeles, he nearly flipped. He eventually calmed down enough to listen as I explained all about Ms. Adelina and how I had to quit the show. I told him I was sorry I left without telling him. That wasn't very responsible of me, I should have let him know there was an emergency before I just left. Trying to keep his cool, Werner asked, no BEGGED, me to come back to Buenos Aires. "Ms. Adelina would want you to," he insisted.

With our conversation spinning round in circles, he realized I wasn't going to change my mind. Before hanging up, he told me to sleep on it and get back to him in the morning.

After a day of tearful prayers at Ms. Adelina's side, I asked my dad to drive me one more place before taking me home. It was Sunday night, and the evening service was just starting. I like Sunday night service, because it's a lot smaller with a mostly younger crowd. I lead worship there a couple of times a month.

I got there just in time, and of course Pastor Ryan handed me his guitar. My friends started clapping as I walked onstage in a jet-lagged daze. I was crazy tired and *completely* stressed, but I was home, doing what I do best, and that felt good.

Sure, it's gonna be hard not being a pop star anymore, no limos, no fancy parties, but up there at God's feet, worshiping Him, that's where I belong.

My Heart

*Why are you downcast, O my soul? Why so disturbed within me?
Put your hope in God for I will yet praise him, my Savior and my
God. (Psalm 42:11)*

Tonight Ms. Adelina's balcony was empty. There was no music, no "Violeta" to comfort me. I would be lying if I told you that didn't hurt. But God is still on His throne, watching over me, and no storm in life is going to ever stop me from worshiping Him.

Good Night, God

On stormy nights and blue sky mornings, let me always praise You. Amen.

That's my prayer. What's yours?

L8R

---

1 COMMENT:

Pastor Ryan said . . .
Notice how they applauded when you took the guitar away from me. Welcome back!
Posted Sunday, 10:32 p.m.

D@y 70: Phone Call

Mood Meter: Juggling Choices

The roller-coaster tale of Izzy Baxter takes yet another shocking turn. Just wait till you hear this.

My dad dropped me off at the hospital early so I could spend the whole day with Ms. Adelina. I brought my laptop so I could do schoolwork, since today was my first day. I hardly got anything done, though. I just couldn't concentrate with everything that was going on.

Ms. Adelina wasn't doing well, and during the night they had put her on a respirator to help her breathe. Not really knowing what else to do, I spent the day crying, praying, and singing to her, you know, just in case she could still hear me. I don't think she could.

Pastor Ryan and his wife, Stephanie, dropped by around noon. I thought that was pretty cool of them. Thanks, guys. They tried to take me to lunch, but I didn't really have much of an appetite, so I passed. Right after they left, my cell phone rang, and that's when things got interesting.

When I saw the call was from Werner, I almost didn't answer it. I thought he was calling to convince me to go back to Argentina again, and I couldn't deal with that today. Reluctantly, I flipped my phone open and waited for the begging to begin.

"Izzy, have you thought about coming back?" he asked.

"I can't come back to Argentina, Werner," I said for the hundredth time. "I need to be in Los Angeles right now."

"Well, how about if the show comes to you?" he asked hopefully. Not understanding what he meant, I listened as he explained how I could perform via a satellite link. While the other contestants performed live in Buenos Aires, I could be performing live from Los Angeles. "Technology can put you in two places at once," he said.

Werner had thrown me for a loop, and I didn't know how to respond. Okay, I totally would want to be back on the show again, but I had Ms. Adelina to take care of, and my homeschooling. On top of that, I hadn't even picked a song or anything. I mean, was it even possible?

"You need to make a decision by tomorrow," he continued. "If you say yes, there are a lot of preparations to make."

With that, he hung up, and now I'm left with yet another life-changing decision to make.

Sigh . . .

My Heart

The fear of the LORD *is the beginning of wisdom; all who follow his precepts have good understanding. (Psalm 111:10)*

Okay, I have had so many decisions to make lately I've become kind of a pro. So, whether you like it or not, here's *Izzy's Step-by-Step Decision Making Wonder Guide*:

Step 1: Go to God for wisdom (pray).
Step 2: Go to the Bible to see what God has to say.
Step 3: Go to your parents and friends and see what they think.
Step 4: Do the right thing!

If you follow these steps, you can't go wrong.

Good Night, God

Lord, Your will be done in everything I do. Amen.
That's my prayer. What's yours?
L8R

---

2 COMMENTS:

Sabine said . . .
Go for it, Iz.
Posted Monday, 6:42 p.m.

James Baxter said . . .
Ditto. 100 percent.
Posted Monday, 8:34 p.m.

Check out the video blog for Day 70:
www.izzyspopstarplan.com/videos.

D@y 71: This Is Me

Mood Meter: Fantastically Me

In case you haven't noticed, I've had a bit of a friendship malfunction with Maddie. She's still been pretty cool to me, but it hasn't really been the same. Totally my fault, since Izzy the pop star had no need for her in Paris. I can't imagine how much that must have hurt her.

So this morning I devoted myself to making things right between us. Given that we weren't really texting each other like we used to, I decided to try a more primitive form of communication, bird mail. My message was simple, "SORRY," penned in pink marker and illustrated with a huge sad face. I shoved the note in the hanging basket and flew it over. Then I texted her. "Did you get my note?" I wanted so badly for her to open her drapes and come out onto her balcony, but she didn't.

I spent the rest of the day crunching calculus problems and wishing it were still summer. Then, right before dinner I heard it, the familiar *thunk* of basket against brick, calling to me like an old friend. BIRD MAIL! I jumped up and ran to the window. Sure enough, the mail I had been waiting for had arrived.

The basket contained a note. "We made something for you. Look on your kitchen table."

I ran into the kitchen, where my dearest friend had placed a wrapped box with an envelope marked "READ FIRST" taped to the top. She must have asked my dad to pick it up or something. I tore open the envelope, eager to hear anything from my long-lost friend. It read:

> To my best bud in the world,
> Awhile back, you asked me who you were. Well, we
> worked on it, and this is what we came up with. This is you.

I was so relieved to hear from the friend I thought I had lost forever, and the leaky faucet of tears was already running before I even opened the box. I lifted open the lid and stared at what was inside.

First, I pulled out a long black skirt, a cool thrift store discovery that only Maddie could have found. It had a pattern of stars on it. A note was attached.

Remember when you used to stare at the stars on your ceiling and dream? God put those dreams in your heart, Izzy. Don't ever forget that. Maddie

Next, I pulled out a string of beautiful pearls.

I wear these when I sing at La Scala. That night I feel so beautiful. I hope they show you how beautiful you are to God. Ms. Adelina

I saw Pastor Ryan's writing on the next note. It was attached to a long-sleeved white designer shirt with a torn-looking collar. Stephanie had written all over the front and back in tiny letters.

These are all the Bible verses you've posted in your blog. Stephanie and I appreciate so much how you have tried to live them out. You have inspired us to love God more and for that we're so thankful. Pastor Ryan

Recognizing the final item in the box, I completely lost it. It was the purple scarf my mother wore during the last year of her life. I hadn't seen it since she died.

It hurts to remember Mom, but that pain is part of who you are. I'm giving you her scarf to remind you that God is going to turn your brokenness into something beautiful. You'll see; one day when we're all together in heaven, everything will make sense again. Dad

Runny-nosed and makeup-free, I ran to the bathroom and tried on my new wardrobe. There, in front of the mirror, without designer labels or a two-thousand-dollar dress, I felt more beautiful than ever.

Right there, I made my decision. I'm going to be there on Performance Night, wearing this outfit.

My Heart

For we are God's workmanship, created in Christ Jesus to do good works, which God prepared in advance for us to do. (Ephesians 2:10)

You are a beautiful work of art, a thing of beauty. God made you, and He doesn't make junk. Everything you are, every dream you have is for a purpose, to serve Him.

Good Night, God

Lord, when I look into the mirror, help me see what You see. Amen.
That's my prayer. What's yours?
L8R

---

4 COMMENTS:

Izzy said . . .
I almost forgot! Thanks everyone!
Posted Tuesday, 10:03 p.m.

Maddie said . . .
You're welcome. ☺
Posted Tuesday, 10:22 p.m.

Pastor Ryan said . . .
I think I found my new calling, fashion design.
Posted Tuesday, 10:30 p.m.

Stephanie said . . .
No problem, Izzy. I had fun working on it.
Posted Tuesday, 10:52 p.m.

Day 72: Life Song

Mood Meter: Radically Rushed

Rush, rush, rushing through my moments now in order to get ready for Performance Night, which is in only TWO DAYS! First thing on the agenda: song choice. Pop Star Plan Rule #46 says it all: "If you're not singing the right song, you shouldn't be singing at all." Choosing the right song, a song that really expresses who I am, is crucial.

Plan A was to sing one of my own songs, but because it would be nearly impossible to teach a backup band something new in such a short time, I trashed that idea. On the way to the hospital in my dad's car, I tried desperately to think of a plan B, but it just wasn't happening.

When we finally arrived, I said bye to my dad and headed to Ms. Adelina's room. By the look on the doctors' faces, I could tell they were worried. I was worried too. Her eyes were still closed; she wasn't talking; she wasn't doing anything but breathing. What if she never woke up? I couldn't imagine life without her music, without her.

In the middle of one of my bedside prayer sessions, a straight-from-heaven idea popped into my head, the perfect song choice. There was a way to bring Ms. Adelina's music back to the neighborhood again. On Performance Night I could sing "Violeta," the song that had been my lullaby for as long as I could remember. I wouldn't need a lot of practice because I knew that melody like the back of my hand, even though it was in Spanish.

I stepped into the hall and flipped open my cell phone. With adrenaline pulsing through my veins like a freight train, I called Werner to tell him the news. He seemed relieved and, at the same time, a bit nervous. Ms. Adelina's balcony was not set up for taping, and he had a lot of preparations to make in a very short time.

"We'll have to get the satellite hookups ready, and a band," he thought out loud.

"About that, um . . . I'd like to use my own musicians, if that's all right with you," I said, explaining the crazy cool idea I had for a backup band. We ended up talking for another twenty minutes or so, ironing out some of the technical details that needed to be taken care of in the next couple of days.

After getting off the phone with him, I made another call, this one to Argentina. There was an old musician friend of mine who needed to book a flight to L.A.

My Heart

Trust in the LORD with all your heart and lean not on your own understanding; in all your ways acknowledge him, and he will make your paths straight. (Proverbs 3:5–6)

Everything seems to be clicking right now. I'm able to be with Ms. Adelina and, at the same time, still be on the show. I've got the PERFECT song to sing, with the perfect backup band. It's like I'm in some kind of heavenly groove or something.

It wasn't like this in Paris. In Paris I was trying to "feel" my way through all my decisions, and it just wasn't happening. This time around, though, I decided to give all my dreams to God, and He's been making my paths straight. Crazy cool!

Good Night, God

Lord, please help me follow Your path for my life, not my own. Amen.

That's my prayer. What's yours?

L8R

---

2 COMMENTS:

Maddie said . . .
Who's the band?
Posted Wednesday, 9:37 p.m.

Izzy said . . .
You'll see. ☺
Posted Wednesday, 9:42 p.m.

Day 73: Lyrics

In case you've been wondering where I've been all day, look up. That's me on the fire escape rehearsing. I've been out here for most of the day and will probably be out here for the next couple of hours or so. Sorry, Mr. McGuire!

Yes, I do know "Violeta" like the back of my hand, *in Spanish*, but the thing is, Werner wants me to sing it in ENGLISH! During our phone call yesterday, he said that since *Pop Star Challenge* has a world audience, I need to sing the song in a language that most people will understand. That's easy for *him* to say. Ms. Adelina wrote "Violeta" herself, and there are no English translations anywhere.

After a brief panic attack, I put my mind to work. Who did I know who spoke Spanish? Ezequiel! Still in my pj's, I frantically ran downstairs to LuLu's to see if the artsy coffeehouse manager could translate. Since I had slept past the morning rush, the place was pretty much empty when I burst through the front door. Ezequiel was more than happy to help. Grabbing a couple of hot chocolates, he pulled up a chair and began deciphering. After about a half hour, he was done and handed me a sheet of LuLu's stationery with my new lyrics on it.

As I began to pour over the words in front of me, I was moved. The song was about a violet. It explained how the tiniest of flowers wasn't as romantic as the rose or as brightly painted as a tulip, but it was the most beautiful in the field because of its heart.

As I began to understand the song's meaning, the tears began to flow. The words of an eighteen-year-old Argentine, from sixty years back, were giving me hope. I mean, I've always been a violet, never the most perfect flower in the field, always messing up. But that doesn't mean that I'm not beautiful. Sure I'm young, but with God's help, I can paint this world a dazzling purple, just like a violet.

My Heart

*The king is enthralled by your beauty; honor him, for he is your
lord. (Psalm 45:11)*

 We don't always feel very beautiful in this life. I mean, this world
has a way of making you feel small and useless sometimes, so take
this verse to heart. God is *enthralled* by how beautiful you are. You're
His child, a work of art, and that's the only opinion that matters.

Good Night, God

Lord, help us shine like violets, knowing that we're beautiful.
Amen.
That's my prayer. What's yours?
L8R

2 COMMENTS:

Maddie said . . .
I'm surprised Mr. McGuire hasn't thrown a bucket of water on you yet!
Posted Thursday, 10:07 p.m.

Izzy said . . .
I know! He's been so quiet lately.
Posted Thursday, 10:15 p.m.

D@y 74: @Performance Night Hollywood

Mood Meter: Sunny at Night

Six o'clock wakeup call this rainy morning. That's when swarms of Quest Studio workers began banging away in Ms. Adelina's apartment. They were setting up for my big satellite performance in eight hours. They set up four different cameras, and even got permission to attach one on the building across the way.

As I listened to them work, I started to get a bit nervous. My musicians hadn't arrived from the airport yet, and we reeeeeeally needed to rehearse. I was relieved to finally hear my backup band stomping up the stairs as I munched on my morning Coconut Crazies. After running to the living room, I flung open the door and there stood Marcelo Farinelli, Ms. Adelina's brother, along with three instrument-toting Argentines. After a round of hugs and coffee, we all headed downstairs to Ms. Adelina's apartment to practice.

As we ran through "Violeta" for the first time, I looked around at the proud, gray-haired musicians surrounding me and began to sob. I wasn't the only one. There was not a dry eye in the room. All of us realized the significance of the moment. Ms. Adelina's band was together again for the first time in over fifty years.

They were true professionals, and the cello, piano, guitar, and accordion sounded amazing. After a two-hour rehearsal, Marcelo and company headed to the hospital to see Ms. Adelina, and I headed back to my apartment for a late lunch/early dinner. After that, I locked myself in my room, closed the blinds, and got into some serious prayer. I wanted to make sure I was ready mentally, and spiritually, for my live performance at exactly 7:27.

A couple of hours before showtime, my dad knocked on my door. The moment of truth had arrived. A makeup artist I didn't recognize did my hair in the kitchen. Then I dressed in the outfit Maddie and my friends had made for me and headed downstairs.

Ms. Adelina's apartment looked beautiful, with candles set in every corner, and her band dressed in worn but elegant suits. After a brief prayer with Marcelo and company, the production manager overseeing the shoot told me how things would work. "At exactly 7:27 p.m., you open the balcony doors and step outside, the musicians begin to play, you sing your song, simple."

Easy for him to say, when 7:25 hit, I was a nervous wreck. While a clock on the wall counted down the seconds, a million thoughts bounced around my brain. What if I forget the words again? What if Mr. McGuire complains IN THE MIDDLE OF MY SONG? I tried to focus on breathing deep, so my voice wouldn't quiver while I sang.

Three, two, one . . . it was time. Mustering all the courage I had, I opened the balcony doors and stepped into the warm California night. I wasn't prepared for what happened next, APPLAUSE, before I had even begun to sing! It started softly but quickly turned into an iron-railing-shaking torrent. It came from every window, fire escape, and balcony. It came from friends, neighbors, and family, who held banners cheering me on. It came from Pastor Ryan and my whole youth group, who were crammed on Maddie's balcony, and Ezequiel, who was looking up from the street below. It even came from Mr. McGuire, who smiled above me.

Over the centuries, there have been millions of standing ovations for millions of pop stars, but there has never been an ovation like this. These were my friends, the ones who truly loved me. They weren't clapping because of what I *did*, because I hadn't even sung yet. They were clapping because of who I am, and for that I will be forever grateful.

After the applause died down, Marcelo nodded, and the music began. I sang confidently as I shared my heart with the world.

> *Violeta, how you paint the fields this evening,*
> *In a land so hard and dry.*
> *You show the world your beauty.*
> *Violeta, smaller than the rose that glistens,*
> *Still, humble as you are,*
> *You speak and mountains listen,*
> *Mí preciosa Violeta.*

The best thing about all this is, I wasn't singing alone tonight. Right after the show, the hospital called. Five miles away, in a lonely hospital room basked in TV light blue, a frail Argentine woman sang along with me. For the first time in over three weeks, Ms. Adelina was awake.

My Heart

And we know that in all things God works for the good of those who love him, who have been called according to his purpose. (Romans 8:28)

As you've probably already figured out, not everything in this life is good. For example, lying to Dad in Paris = bad thing. Ms. Adelina having a stroke = bad thing. But the cool thing about being a Christian is that God can take all the bad things that happen and flip them over into something good. I can see how He's been doing that in my own life. My failure in Paris caused me to get closer to my dad and to God. Ms. Adelina's stroke caused me to look for Marcelo, and now he's in Los Angeles by his sister's side. So next time you're looking at a downside, just wait; God is going to work it into something lovely.

Good Night, God

Lord, thanks for turning "all things" into something good. Amen.
That's my prayer. What's yours?
L8R

---

3 COMMENTS:

Anders said . . .
No way! I cannot believe how well you pulled that off. Way to go, sis.
Posted Friday, 10:34 p.m.

Stephanie said . . .
I'm speechless, Izzy, absolutely speechless.
Posted Friday, 10:54 p.m.

James Baxter said . . .
I can't believe that was my little girl out there, the one who used to drive her brother crazy by singing "The Itsy Bitsy Spider" all day long. I'm proud of you, Iz.
Posted Friday, 11:07 p.m.

Day 75: @Vote Night Buenos Aires

Mood Meter: Jumpy

Tonight had to be one of the most fun nights I have ever had. I hosted a Vote Night party for all of my friends and family at LuLu's. All my youth group friends were there, and Ezequiel was handing out cookies and smoothies, for FREE! Quest Studios brought in this huge TV so we could watch the Vote Night show in style. They also set up another satellite feed so that while the show was going on live in Argentina, they could jump to scenes of me watching with my buds in Hollywood. Crazy cool.

After hanging out for about an hour or so, it was time, five o'clock (ten in Argentina). We scooted our chairs around the big screen and listened as the *International Pop Star Challenge* theme music filled the room.

Sean Moore opened the show with a recap of last night's performances. I leaned forward in my seat. I hadn't watched any of the other contestants' performances, and I was dying to see what I was up against.

Miklos, of course, sang this outrageous heavy metal song. It wasn't kind to the ears, but it was Miklos. Next came the performance I was the most interested in, Etienne's. I was surprised at how worn out he looked. He usually uses up every inch of the stage and interacts with the crowd, but not tonight. Tonight he looked as stiff as one of those statues we saw at the Louvre museum in Paris. From the look and sound of his Buenos Aires performance, I was worried he'd be on his way back home after tonight's show.

Then Atsumi came on wearing a gorgeously long white dress. She sang a beautiful ballad, half in English and half in Japanese. Her song had something that Etienne's lacked—passion.

Before the recap of my song came on, they did something different. The theater lights dimmed, and they showed a short film of Ms. Adelina's life. They showed how she grew up poor and became an opera star. They showed black-and-white footage of her performing at some of the greatest opera houses in the world. Then the narrator spoke about her stroke and how she had been in a coma for three weeks. When the theater lights came back on, a happier scene flashed on the screen. It was Ms. Adelina, live from the hospital. She was sitting up in bed and talking to me! "Thank you for you prayers and you love. Good luck tonight, Preciosa," she said feebly as the audience in Argentina gave her a standing ovation that seemed to last forever.

After showing my balcony performance in its entirety, it was time for the results. As an official-looking studio employee handed the sealed envelope to Sean Moore, I hoped with all my heart that Atsumi and I would be the ones voted through to the New York City finals—no offense, Miklos.

First came Miklos. Sean said, "You sang 'Lightning Fire.' Giuseppe Rossi said it was 'the soundtrack to a nightmare.' Aiko Mae said it 'wasn't her style.' The world has voted and . . . I'm sorry, you are heading home tonight." With that news, Miklos waved sadly to the audience and walked offstage.

Next, Atsumi and Edina were called to center stage. As a spotlight, shone down on them, Sean Moore continued, "Edina, your performance of 'Sounds of Love' was, according to Giuseppe, 'missing something.' Aiko said, 'Hopefully the world will vote on your past performances and forget tonight's.' Marshall Phillips said one word, 'Dull.' The world has voted, and Atsumi, you are moving on to the finals." I stood up and cheered when I heard that news, and then suddenly felt a wave of panic hit me when I realized that my own pop star fate would be decided in the next couple of minutes.

That left me and Etienne. I could feel a camera focusing in on me as Sean began to speak the words that could possibly change my life. "Izzy Baxter, you sang 'Violeta.' The judges were moved to tears by your performance. Aiko said, 'Tonight you shared your heart with the world, and it was beautiful.' The world has voted and . . . Etienne Rousseau, you are heading back to France."

See me onscreen!
www.izzyspopstarplan.com/videos.
Click on Day 75.

For a few seconds, what Sean Moore said didn't register. All I could think of was Etienne losing, and that was tragically sad. But then, all of a sudden, as I was being crushed by hugs and confetti rained down on my head, I realized what had just happened. I'M GOING TO NEW YORK! I'm not much of a screamer, but tonight I screamed, in front of an audience of millions. In fact, we all screamed and celebrated for the rest of the night.

I'm joyfully exhausted!

My Heart

He fulfills the desires of those who fear him; he hears their cry and saves them. (Psalm 145:19)

A long time ago a little girl with a hairbrush microphone in her hand dreamed of one day being a pop star. She thought she was the only one watching herself sing in front of that mirror that day. But she wasn't, God was watching too. And that little dream of hers? Ten years later, He still remembered.

Good Night, God

Lord, I really wanted this, and You gave it to me. Thanks so much! Amen.

That's my prayer. What's yours?

L8R

---

1 COMMENT:

James Baxter said . . .

I hate to break it to you, Iz, but the walls of that bathroom are pretty thin. I think the entire apartment building knew about those pop star plans of yours.

Posted Saturday, 11:34 p.m.

PART 5

Hello, New York

I got a heart that beats,
And I've got a soul in me.
I've still got some life in me yet,
So I'm gonna worship You until my last breath.

"SING"—IZZY BAXTER

D@y 76: Update

Mood Meter: Full Speed Ahead

Packing, packing, and packing some more! I'm starting to become a pro traveler and have my carry-on bag perfectly organized: MP3 player in the outside pocket for easy access during flight, a bag of sour ropes in top, and my mini travel Bible for up-in-the-clouds time with God. All geared up for the Big Apple!

Why am I packing, and blogging, at three in the morning? WAY TOO MUCH ADRENALINE rushing through my veins, that's why. Well, since I can't sleep, let's go ahead and make this "Day 76" and I'll give you an update on some people you're probably wondering about!

Anders: He left for Stanford this morning . . . sniff, sniff. Since Dad is going to New York with me, Anders ended up carpooling with a friend. It was depressing to walk by his empty room just now. He's gonna come home for Thanksgiving in a couple of months, but that's two months too long! Now for some happy Anders news. He and Atsumi are officially dating, but with him in northern California and her waaaaaaay over in Asia, there won't be many dates. Poor guy.

Maddie: Maddie and I are best buds again after our little rough patch. After getting the outfit, I headed over to her apartment and we talked for, like, three hours. Most of that time was spent with me apologizing, and she was so cool about everything. That's Maddie for you.

Ms. Adelina: My dad called the hospital last night. After a nurse heard her singing, she sat up in bed and talked a little. She's not strong enough to walk yet, and the doctors are still concerned about her heart, but she's definitely doing better. Keep praying. Her brother decided to stick around until she recovers. With Marcelo by her side, I don't feel so bad heading off to New York.

Etienne: Okay, check this out. About an hour ago, I got not one but TWO texts from Etienne. The first one said, "Congrats. U deserve this," and the second one, which came five minutes later, said, "Been reading the Bible U gave me. Thx 4 being U." I'm not sure what to make of this, but it all sounds pretty cool to me.

So that's the scoop, my friends. Next up, NEW YORK CITY!

My Heart
Still other seed fell on good soil. It came up and yielded a crop, a hundred times more than was sown. (Luke 8:8)

It's so exciting to hear how God is working in Etienne's heart. I mean, he's actually reading the Bible I gave him! Crazy cool! Powerful things begin to happen when we share God's love with someone. It's like planting a seed. We may not see anything growing right away, but when we plant God's Word in a person's heart, something powerful begins to happen.

Good Night, God
Lord, please show us how to plant seeds of Your love wherever You place us. Amen.

That's my prayer. What's yours?

L8R

---

2 COMMENTS:

Sabine said . . .

First question: What were you doing up in the middle of the night?!
Second question: Isn't Etienne going to see all the stuff you've been putting in your blog?
Posted Sunday, 7:43 a.m.

Izzy said . . .

I couldn't sleep, and no, NEVER! There's no way I'm ever giving him the password. I'd be crazy embarrassed if he read some of the things I've been writing about him. Nope, this blog is for close friends only.
Posted Sunday, 8:17 a.m.

D@y 77: Happy SunMorning

Mood Meter: Joyfully Drenched

This portion of Izzy Baxter's life is being brought to you live from the first-class cabin of Transamerica flight 885 headed nonstop to the Big Apple. You know, I'm kind of getting used to traveling first class, thanks to Quest Studios. If you weren't at church this morning, I have great news to tell you.

Over the last couple of weeks or so, I've been thinking. I want my faith to be out there, for the whole world to see. I want God and everyone else to know that "I, Izzy Baxter, love God with all my heart, soul, and mind." Then one day it came to me, the perfect way to express my all-out commitment to God, getting baptized. I've been wanting to do that for a while, ever since I became a Christian at family camp when I was eight. But for some reason I never really got around to it, so this morning I took the plunge, literally.

It happened during ten o'clock service. After worship, Pastor Ryan and my dad walked up to the Jacuzzi-looking thing they have at the back of the stage, and there in front of all my church friends, I stepped into the water for one of the most amazing moments with God ever. Of course, my dad had to go and give me this huge hug, which sent us both into tears.

Then Pastor Ryan began asking the questions he always asks when he does baptisms. When he asked me, "Izzy, do you believe that Jesus is the Son of the living God?" I answered, "Yes!" so emphatically that he actually laughed. I didn't mind, being that this was a happy thing. Then he dunked me under, and that was that. When I rose out of the water, everyone at church was clapping, even Kenji and Miya, whom Quest Studios sent to film the whole thing.

Hey, maybe they'll show the tape during the finals. Then the whole world will know that IZZY BAXTER LOVES JESUS!

A totally perfect day, except for the fact that Anders wasn't there. I'm already starting to miss him.

My Heart

As soon as Jesus was baptized, he went up out of the water. At that moment heaven was opened, and he saw the Spirit of God descending like a dove and lighting on him. And a voice from heaven said, "This is my Son, whom I love; with him I am well pleased." (Matthew 3:16–17)

When Jesus was baptized, God told Him how much He loved Him, and how pleased He was with Him. That was before Jesus had even started His ministry. This shows that God loved His Son because of *who He was*, not because of *what He did*. God loves you in that same way. He loves you not because of what you've done for Him, but because you are you. That's real love.

Good Night, God

Lord, thank You for washing me clean so that every day can be new. Amen.
That's my prayer. What's yours?
L8R

---

3 COMMENTS:

Ms. Adelina said . . .
Fly safe, Preciosa, and don't worry about me. Margaret, my nurse, she help me so I can still read you blog.
Posted Sunday, 8:41 p.m.

Anders said . . .
I'm sorry I missed it, Iz. Dad's gonna send me a DVD of the whole thing. I'll call you after I watch.
Posted Sunday, 9:43 p.m.

Stephanie said . . .
So excited for you, Izzy!
Posted Sunday, 10:12 p.m.

Day 78: Taxis and Ice Cream

Mood Meter: Awkward

Got to New York late last night and checked in to our hotel, the TriStar International, right next to Central Park. I didn't see much of the city on our way downtown because I was in a deep sleep until we pulled up to the front of the hotel. My dad had to shake me awake when the limo stopped, and I'm sure I didn't look very happy when the paparazzi (yes, they're back) started snapping away.

Needless to say, I'm exhausted. Atsumi looked pretty worn out too when I met her in the hotel restaurant for ice cream today. I had been looking forward to seeing her ever since I left Argentina, but our reunion was kind of disappointing. The whole hour I spent with her was kind of awkward. There was this uncomfortable silence in the room, like we didn't know what to say to each other. Maybe it's because we were both totally drained, or maybe it's because we're competing against each other for the title. She asked about Anders, so we talked a little about him. Then she told me about how sad Miklos, Edina, and Etienne were after being sent home. But we didn't really get into the heart-to-heart stuff like we usually do.

I have so much in common with that girl, it's crazy. We're both songwriters, we've both dreamed of making it in the music business since we were kids, and now the two of us want to win *International Pop Star Challenge* more than ever. I hope our similarities don't end up pulling us apart.

I tried to pay for our ice cream, but the waiter, who recognized us from the show, wouldn't let us. Being a pop star has its perks, I guess. Too bad being a star doesn't make friendship any easier.

My Heart
A friend loves at all times, and a brother is born for adversity.
(Proverbs 17:17)

Okay, so today was a bad day, but I'm not going to write off my friendship with Atsumi because of that. Friendships go through seasons. Sometimes you're glued together like Siamese twins, and sometimes you need some space. That's just the way it works. But in the end, true friends are able to rise above all that. Through bad mood mornings, through disagreements, through seasons apart from each other, "a friend loves at all times."

Good Night, God
Lord, help me be a good friend even when it's awkward. Amen.
That's my prayer. What's yours?
L8R

---

2 COMMENTS:

Maddie said . . .
Friendships are worth the messiness, though.
Posted Monday, 4:14 p.m.

Izzy said . . .
Definitely!
Posted Monday, 9:05 p.m.

D⋈y 79: @Challenge Night New York

Mood Meter: Stylin'

Tonight's Challenge Night show was over-the-top cool. Radio City Music Hall was packed to the rafters with fans, and there was an awesome lineup of performers. The best part was that I didn't have to perform, so I could just relax and enjoy the show. I even dressed casually cool, brown leather boots, ripped jeans, down-to-my-knees cotton top, long cross necklace, and *lots* of bracelets.

Werner really outdid himself this time. The night opened with this guy named Eddie Lewis, who I guess was a famous rocker in the fifties, fun! Then they showed clips of people's audition tapes for the show; some were pretty horrible sounding. After that, Laila and the Ravonettes performed their hit from the sixties, "I Need You." They were kind of old, but their vocals were still pretty tight.

Following that they showed another video montage of all these people wishing us luck. It was amazing! There were people from India to Australia who knew who we were. In Kyoto, Japan, there was an arena full of people watching the show live! I could tell Atsumi was touched. After that, the show really took off, with bands like C&C Music Factory from the seventies, Morning Fire representing the eighties, and Boys on the Run from the nineties.

Then came the biggest surprise of the night, for me at least. With one decade left to go, the lights went low and a familiar chord progression started chiming from the speakers. I instantly recognized the song. It was Trevor Carson and the Moon Babies. They had reworked "Cellular," off their last album, and it sounded awesome. I was totally blown away. When they were finished, I couldn't help but stand up and cheer along with the rest of the audience.

Of course, they waited until the last ten minutes of the hourlong show to give us our challenge. We nervously stood up and took our place center stage. In typical fashion, the music got all dramatic as someone brought out not one, but six envelopes. Arm and arm, Atsumi and I listened intently as Marshall Phillips began to explain our task.

"Tonight you heard some of the world's best music from the last sixty years," he began. "Rockabilly, disco, alternative, you heard it all.

For your final challenge, you will be celebrating the last six decades of song."

Aiko took over from there. "In just a moment you will each select one of these six envelopes. Inside you will find a note. That note will determine which decade you will sing from. If you are not happy with your selection, you may trade with your opponent. The choice is yours."

Giuseppe, who held the envelopes in his hands, went next. "Izzy, since you had the highest number of votes in the last round, you may select first."

I nervously grabbed the envelope in the middle. A spotlight beamed down on me as I tore it open and saw my fate, the sixties, not my favorite, but doable.

Next came Atsumi. Her note said "modern," which meant that she could sing anything recent.

Sean Moore wrapped up the night with some pretty incredible news. Our final performance is going to be at Madison Square Garden! Crazy cool!

My Heart

Then I heard what sounded like a great multitude, like the roar of rushing waters and like loud peals of thunder, shouting: "Hallelujah! For our Lord God Almighty reigns." (Revelation 19:6)

Seeing all those fans from around the world cheering today reminded me of this verse. At the end of time, when the devil is finally defeated, there will be no more pain or suffering in the world, and people will praise the right things, not pop stars or athletes, but God, because He is the One who deserves all glory and honor and praise.

Good Night, God

Lord, You deserve all our praise and worship. We love You. Amen. That's my prayer. What's yours?
L8R

---

1 COMMENT:

Pastor Ryan said . . .
Yeah, isn't it weird that people who can hit a ball real far with a stick get more praise than God sometimes?
Posted Tuesday, 8:54 p.m.

Day 80: Trade?

Mood Meter: Perfectly Puzzled

To trade or not to trade? That is the question. Atsumi approached me in the lobby today and asked if I wanted to trade decades with her. I could have the modern era, and she would take the sixties. HUGE DECISION! I told her I would think about it and get back to her tomorrow.

So that's what I've been doing all day, thinking about it. I have to admit, I'm totally not into the sixties. I don't think I've ever downloaded a sixties song in my life. But . . . I don't want to trade with Atsumi for one simple reason: the Beatles are from the sixties, and if that Beatles-obsessed girl sings one of their songs, she is going to absolutely destroy me in the finals. On the other hand, is winning *International Pop Star Challenge* worth destroying our friendship? HELP! Decision meltdown approaching!

I'm totally torn. I mean, I'm in this thing to win it. I knew going in that if I wanted to make it in this business, I would have to make some tough decisions. I mean, Pop Star Plan Rule #25 says it pretty clearly: "The pop world is a jungle, so roar like a lion." Atsumi, of all people, should understand that. She wants to win it as much as I do. If she's a true friend, she'll stick around even if I decide not to trade.

Then again, I can't be so obsessed with making it in this business that I end up selfishly hurting the people I love. Been there, done that, don't ever want to make that mistake again.

Excuse me, I need to go find a rooftop and start praying.

My Heart

He answered: "Love the Lord your God with all your heart and with all your soul and with all your strength and with all your mind"; and, "Love your neighbor as yourself." (Luke 10:27)

"Remember, life isn't only Izzy." That's what Ms. Adelina told me awhile back. She's right, you know. I'm not the center of the universe. Sure the world keeps telling me to look out for number one, but God tells a different story. In all my decisions, God wants me to look at the needs of others as well as my own. I guess a good question for me to ask is, "If I were in Atsumi's shoes, what would I want my friend to do?"

Good Night, God

Lord, in all my decisions, help me love You with all my heart, and love my neighbor as myself. Amen.

That's my prayer. What's yours?

L8R

---

2 COMMENTS:

Pastor Ryan said . . .
Keep praying, Iz. God will tell you what to do.
Posted Wednesday, 5:43 p.m.

Izzy said . . .
He always does. ☺
Posted Wednesday, 10:31 p.m.

Day 81: Skyscraper High

Mood Meter: Cloud-Hopping

Being a pop star does have its perks. Check this out. This morning I went down to the lobby to ask the concierge if she knew of any rooftops where I could do my schoolwork, play my guitar, and generally just enjoy the view. I thought she would just give me directions to a building nearby that had an observation deck or something, but she had other plans.

About thirty minutes after asking her, I got this call in my room, from the concierge. "Your limo is waiting downstairs," she said. Pleasantly surprised, I shoved my schoolbooks in my backpack, grabbed my guitar case, and headed down.

The next thing I know, I'm limo-ing down Lexington Avenue toward the Chrysler Building. After a quick ride, the chauffer pulled up to the curb where a Quest Studios production assistant was waiting. She guided me past security and toward one of the building's thirty-two elevators. On the way up I commented, "I thought the Chrysler building wasn't open to tourists."

The assistant smiled and answered, "To tourists, no. To pop stars, yes!"

The elevator stopped at the 67th floor, the doors opened, and I was staring at a beautifully abandoned art deco floor with wall-to-wall windows. The view literally knocked me back a few steps. We were actually standing above some low-lying clouds! "This floor used to be called the Cloud Club," lectured my studio babysitter, "the most happening place in town, fifty years ago." She went on to explain how huge stars like Clark Gable and Katharine Hepburn used to hang out here back in the day.

"Just call downstairs when you're done," she said, stepping back into the elevator. I couldn't believe what was happening. I had the whole floor to myself! Staring at the New York skyline from my sky-high perch, I began to pray, thanking God for all the amazing things He'd blessed me with over the last few months.

Suddenly, this incredibly clear thought came to me. God's blessed me with so much, and now I want to be a blessing to others.

I picked up my cell phone and dialed Atsumi's number. There was a trade I needed to make.

My Heart

But seek first his kingdom and his righteousness, and all these things will be given to you as well. (Matthew 6:33)

I feel good about my decision. Atsumi was through-the-roof thrilled that I was willing to trade. She gave me this huge hug in the lobby tonight, and things seem back to normal between us. She's gonna blow everyone away with some Beatles song, I know it, and I have no idea what song to sing, but that doesn't bother me anymore. I did the right thing today, and God is going to take care of the rest.

Good Night, God

Lord, help me always try my best to please You first, knowing that You'll take care of everything else. Amen.

That's my prayer. What's yours?

L8R

---

1 COMMENT:

Ms. Adelina said . . .
Do what's right and you will never fail.
Posted Thursday, 7:02 p.m.

Day 82: Can't Believe You Love Me

Mood Meter: Sweet Like a Lollipop

I woke up with one thing on my mind, Performance Night. Werner wanted our song choices by tomorrow, and I had no idea what to sing. I made arrangements to use the 67th floor of the Chrysler Building again. I figured another day in the clouds with my guitar would somehow lead me to the right song.

First, though, I needed food. My dad and I headed to this coffee place across the street for a muffin and smoothie breakfast. That's when I saw HER—Renee, the show's publicist who nearly ruined my life in Paris. Trying my best to be forgiving, I walked over to her table to say hi.

"Pick a song yet?" she asked with an everything-is-fine smile.

"No, going to work on that today," I answered.

"You *do* know that you can sing one of your own songs, don't you?" she said.

"Really?" I asked in shock. "I thought I had to pick from the current decade."

"Izzy, anything you write is current," she continued as she gathered her things to leave. "You're a talented songwriter. I would seriously consider singing one of your own songs." With those last words of advice, she left.

Happily stunned, I sat down on her now vacant chair. The idea of singing one of my own songs opened up a world of possibilities. I scarfed down a chocolate-chip muffin, hugged my dad good-bye, and headed across the street to my waiting limo.

By the time I got to my 67th floor perch, the clouds had opened up and rain was pouring down on the city. Using raindrops as my rhythm section, I started to play. I could tell right away that a new song was about to be born, and I began singing the first words that came to my heart.

> *I can't believe, I can't believe You love me,*
> *That You're turning my failures into something lovely.*

During these last three months, I had been far from perfect. I had messed up, I had doubted God, I had fallen, and each time God's was there, picking me up, comforting me, blessing me, even though I didn't deserve it. I began to praise Him and let Him know that I appreciated all that He'd done for me.

> *Now all I really want to do is give this broken heart to You,*
> *'Cause I can't believe, I can't believe You love me.*

You know, I've been singing for a lot of people lately, for producers, for hospital-bound kids, for Ms. Adelina, for myself, but this time I'm going to sing for someone else. On Performance Night I'm going to sing my newest song to God.

My Heart
I will praise the LORD all my life; I will sing praise to my God as long as I live. (Psalm 146:2)

I can't believe God loves us! It's absolutely incredible. He watches over us and cares about everything that's going on in our lives. He's the King above all kings, the Maker of all the stars and galaxies, and still He wants to have a relationship with us! That's why He deserves our praise.

Good Night, God
Lord, we praise You for Your awesome love. Amen.
That's my prayer. What's yours?
L8R

---

2 COMMENTS:

Maddie said . . .
Lord, I praise You that school is working out well!
Posted Friday, 6:37 p.m.

Ms. Adelina said . . .
I praise You for another day of life.
Posted Friday, 7:02 p.m.

Day 83: Resistance

Mood Meter: Feet Planted

No rooftop relaxing today. With only six days left till Performance Night, it was all work and no play. I headed to Metro Pointe Rehearsal Studios at about nine this morning, and besides a quick lunch break, have pretty much practiced all day. It's almost 11:00 p.m. in New York right now, and I'm still here! So much for finishing my social studies assignment. Sorry, Dad!

The whole morning was spent teaching "I Can't Believe You Love Me" to my wonderfully amazing backup band. The guitar player came up with this awesome riff. I can't wait till you hear it! After lunch, we all gathered in this huge rehearsal room to do a low-key run-through of the show. Everyone was really relaxed, even Werner, who tends to be uptight on Performance Night weeks.

Atsumi was up first. She, of course, sang a Beatles song, "Let It Be." A small orchestra accompanied her, and it sounded over-the-moon amazing. Everyone in the room, technicians, stagehands, and assistants, gave her a standing ovation. Clapping wildly along with the others, one thought kept running through my mind: *I'm gonna lose!*

I was supposed to go next, but there was some confusion about the order of events for the evening, so I had to wait for a half hour or so until Sean Moore and Werner finally worked it out. Smiling, I eventually took my place in front of the judges' table and began singing away. Like Atsumi, I got a pretty good response from everyone there.

As I headed back to the folding chair that had been my home for the last couple of hours, Marshall, the American judge, called me over. "Izzy, nice song," he said. "Can I see your lyrics?"

"Sure," I said, pulling out my song notebook. He scanned the page, stopping to look closely at the bridge.

> *On the cross, You took my shame;*
> *I don't deserve the love You gave.*
> *You won my heart, You took my place,*
> *So I can sing this song of Grace.*

"This is a religious song," he said.

"Yeah, I guess you could say that," I answered, wondering what he was getting at.

Putting his hand on my shoulder, he lectured, "Izzy, not everyone is a Christian. Save songs like this for church. You've worked so hard to get this far, I would hate to see you blow it because of your song choice."

The whole conversation left a bitter taste in my mouth. I started thinking, *Will singing that song hurt my chances?* Right then and there, I made a decision. The next time we do a run-through, I'm going to sing the bridge louder than ever!

My Heart

I am not ashamed of the gospel, because it is the power of God for the salvation of everyone who believes. (Romans 1:16)

I'm not going to be ashamed of singing my song to God on Performance Night. I never want to be ashamed of the gospel, even if it costs me votes or my career. I mean, I love God. He's my dearest friend and Father, and I'm not going to hide that. I'm sorry, Marshall Phillips, but that's the way it's gonna be.

Good Night, God

Lord, help me stand boldly for the gospel. Amen.

That's my prayer. What's yours?

L8R

---

1 COMMENT:

James Baxter said . . .
That's my girl.
Posted Saturday, 11:16 p.m.

D@y 84: Harlem

Mood Meter: Alive and Kicking

Step right up, folks. Izzy and Atsumi's ten-hour tour of the Big Apple is about to set sail!

First stop, Harlem.

Being that it was Sunday, Atsumi and I wanted to find a church to go to in the morning. We thought it would be cool to attend Eastside Baptist in Harlem. They have this awesome hundred-member gospel choir that I saw on TV once, and I thought it would be crazy cool to see them live. They didn't disappoint, and neither did the pastor. The Reverend James T. Harper, a seventy-year-old African-American, gave one of the most passionate sermons about God's love I have ever heard. At one point he kept repeating, "Do you believe that God loves you? Do you really *believe* that God loves you? Do you BELIEVE that God loves you?"

By the time he had finished, Atsumi and I were up on our feet with the rest of the congregation shouting, "Hallelujah, we believe it!"

Next, we taxied over to Dylan's Candy Bar on the Upper East Side. That place is huge! Three stories of wall-to-wall candy. You don't want to know how much candy I dumped into that little plastic bag of mine, pretty embarrassing.

After grabbing some hot dogs from a street vendor, we walked to Central Park. It was a surprisingly sunny day, so the place was packed. We didn't mind, though; all the laughing kids made a great happy-day soundtrack for us as we strolled along jogging paths and people watched.

At one point, Atsumi grabbed my hand and pulled me to this huge playground. With the paparazzi hiding who knows where, I was a little paranoid at first, but seeing Atsumi's smile as she started swing-ing made me relax a little, and I joined her. We laughed as we tried to see how high we could go. We were just two kids again, playing on a playground, and that felt good.

After attempting a synchronized swing jump, we ended up in a pile of sore knees and laughter. Because of our major giggle attack, getting up seemed impossible, so we decided to crash there for a while.

"I think you gonna win," said Atsumi when things calmed down.

"Are you kidding?" I said. "Your version of 'Let It Be' makes Paul McCartney look like a total amateur."

Then, getting serious, she said, "Izzy, no matter what happens, we still be friends, right?"

Giving her a hug, I answered, "No matter what."

Check out the video.
www.izzyspopstarplan.com/videos.
Day 84

My Heart

How good and pleasant it is when brothers live together in unity! (Psalm 133:1)

Today was a crazy cool day. The awkwardness between Atsumi and me melted away, and we were just two friends hanging out again. It felt so good. God likes it when friends work through their rough patches, and I like it too.

Good Night, God

Lord, help us work through our differences so we can live in unity with each other. Amen.

That's my prayer. What's yours?

L8R

---

1 COMMENT:

Maddie said . . .

Okay, hearing about that candy store gave us both a sweet tooth, so Sabine and I convinced our moms to take us to the Candy Cellar after church tonight. Fun! Wish you were here.

Posted Sunday, 9:02 p.m.

D@y 85: Circus of Questions

Mood Meter: Totally Talked Out

Another manic Monday has come and gone! Three hours of interviews in the morning, four hours of rehearsal after lunch. My voice is worn out from all that talking and singing.

It all started with an eight o'clock breakfast meeting with Werner, Renee, and some of the technical crew. Then we headed down the hall to this huge banquet room Quest Studios had reserved for "media day." That's the day when all the magazines and TV stations from around the world get one-on-one time with us.

After the first few journalists, the questions all started sounding the same. "What song will you be singing?" "What's your game plan for the finals?" "How has fame changed you?" And of course they asked the classic, "Are you and Etienne still seeing each other?" I've become a pro at answering that one: "I'm still a bit young for the whole dating scene, but we're definitely still friends." I wonder, though. Are we still friends? Sigh.

At noon, with a line of reporters still waiting at the door, Renee ended media day, and we headed to the rehearsal studio. My backup band and I must have gone over "I Can't Believe You Love Me" about twenty times before we declared it tight as a drum.

From there, I headed over to wardrobe, where Christine had a surprise for me. After going over my hair and makeup for the big night, she pulled out a skirt, leggings, black boots, and short military-looking jacket with an incredible hand-painted shirt for underneath. When you look at the front closely, you can see a cross. Totally unique!

"I thought you would like that shirt, being a Christian and all." She said smiling.

"I love it!" I answered and gave her a huge hug. "Thanks for everything, Christine."

"No, thank you, Iz," she said. "Hanging out with you has taught me a lot."

With that, my final wardrobe consultation with Christine was done, and I headed toward the parking lot, excited to just go to my hotel room and crash. Before I could make it through the front door, I heard a familiar voice call my name, Marshall Phillips.

"Have you thought about what I told you the other day?" he said.

"Yes, I have," I answered. "I'm sticking with my song choice. Sorry."

"Don't say sorry to me," he answered with a roll of his eyes. "You sing that religious song on Friday, and it's your career that's going to take a hit."

Not really knowing what else to say, I thanked him for the advice and headed to my waiting limo.

I have to admit, his words do scare me a bit. What if I lose because of my song?

My Heart

For we are to God the aroma of Christ among those who are being saved and those who are perishing. To the one we are the smell of death; to the other, the fragrance of life. (2 Corinthians 2:15–16)

When we live out our Christian faith, some people are going to like what they see in us, like Christine and Etienne. They'll be interested, and maybe even start asking questions. We're like a sweet-smelling flower to them. But others, like Marshall Phillips, aren't going to like our faith at all. When we show them God's love, they'll start feeling bad about the way they're living and maybe even get upset. We can't freak out when that happens. It comes with the territory. As Christians, we'll never be able to please everyone.

Good Night, God

Lord, help me lovingly live out my faith, no matter what people think. Amen.

That's my prayer. What's yours?

L8R

---

1 COMMENT:

Pastor Ryan said . . .

You got it right, Izzy. We will never be able to please everyone. Look at how many feathers Jesus ruffled.

Posted Monday, 8:04 p.m.

Day 86: Fave Five

Mood Meter: Nostalgic

In four days, my *International Pop Star Challenge* journey will come to an end. What a trip! I spent the day working on another list, Izzy's *Pop Star Challenge* Fave Five. Here it goes:

Favorite Celebrity Meeting: Back in Paris, at the perfume launch party, I got to meet Elaine Burton. A lot of the guests didn't recognize her because she hasn't been in any films for a while, but I did. Anders and I are crazy about old musicals, and I knew right away that she was the one who danced with Fred Astaire in *Fifty Nights*. I got her autograph on a napkin!

Funniest Moment: When Anders got stuck on the Tokyo subway, I nearly died laughing. We were at Harajuku station and our subway had just pulled up to the platform. The train was PACKED! Anders found a way to squeeze in, but there was no way that Atsumi and I were going to even attempt it. While Anders tried to convince us that there was room, the door slid closed and off he went. I wish I had a picture of his face, crushed up against the window as the train pulled away. It was hilarious.

Favorite Place Visited: If I had to choose between Tokyo and New York, I would probably say New York. The whole city has this trendy vibe that I love, and the view from my Chrysler Building rehearsal space has inspired me to write some really cool tunes. I'm loving it here.

Favorite Performance by Someone Else: I have to say that Colleen Leary's Tokyo performance was one of the most beautiful, and heart-breaking, performances I have ever seen. That British girl really spilled her heart out on that stage. It was sad but sweet at the same time. We were all shocked when she didn't make it past the first round.

My Heart

Know therefore that the LORD your God is God; he is the faithful God, keeping his covenant of love to a thousand generations of those who love him and keep his commands. (Deuteronomy 7:9)

Now to the last thing on my list, my favorite "me" performance: I bet you're all thinking that I'm going to say my balcony performance of "Violeta" was my favorite, but you're wrong. "Violeta" was definitely up there, but I would have to say that singing "How Can I Keep from Singing?" at the audition was tops on my list. That song means so much to me since it's the one my mom used to sing to me all the time. It even means more to me now. In everything I've gone through in these last few months, God has never, not once, let me down. How could I ever keep from singing?

Good Night, God

Lord, help me sing for You always and forever. Amen.
That's my prayer. What's yours?
L8R

---

4 COMMENTS:

Anders said . . .
Hey, don't laugh. I spent fifteen minutes crushed like that before I was
finally able to get off. ☺
Posted Tuesday, 7:34 p.m.

Izzy said . . .
Hey, at least we stuck around until you were able to find your way back.
By the way, I MISS U!
Posted Tuesday, 8:26 p.m.

Anders said . . .
I miss you too, but I'll see you on Friday.
Posted Tuesday, 10:47 p.m.

Izzy said . . .
WHAT!!!!!!
Posted Tuesday, 10:57 p.m.

D@y 87: Old Friends

Mood Meter: Butterfly Heart

Dress rehearsal today, at Madison Square Garden! The set for the finals looks totally awesome. I got goose bumps just thinking about singing in the same arena where people like Frank Sinatra and Elvis have performed. Crazy cool!

After our sound checks, Atsumi and I were stunned to see all eighteen other *International Pop Star Challenge* finalists making their way onstage. Colleen, Miklos, Etienne, they were all there. Werner had brought them all back for the finals! We cheered as they sang a group number they had been working on. Seeing Etienne was completely awkward at first, and painful, but after giving each other a quick hug, things felt better, well, at least a tiny bit better.

Four hours later we were off to Orpheum, the hippest restaurant in town, for a good-bye dinner. After the main course, Werner banged his spoon on his glass to get our attention. It was time for the "Werner Awards," the awards he gives his cast and crew at the end of each season.

First came the "America Rock and Roll" Award, which of course went to Miklos, who had driven us crazy with that phrase over the last couple of months. He laughed as Werner handed him an American flag–painted electric guitar.

Next came the "Top of Pop" award, a golden microphone, which went to Etienne, whose newest single had become the number one download in Europe. He actually seemed pretty shy as he went up to collect his prize.

After several more awards were given out, and the ceremony neared its end, Werner held up the last award of the night, a small, diamond, angel-wing pendant. "Though this person is one of the youngest contestants we have ever had on the show, her passion and sincerity have moved us all. Izzy Baxter, to you I give the Angel Award."

A bit embarrassed, I walked up to Werner's table and thanked him as he handed me my prize. Before I could go back to my seat, he grabbed my hand and made one final announcement. "Putting on a show like this, we need all the help we can get," he said with a smile. "Izzy, would you like to say a prayer for us?"

Shocked at his request, I smiled awkwardly, said "sure," and began to pray. I asked that God would show His love to everyone in the cast and crew, and that He would help make Performance Night the best ever.

There were a few amens at the end of my prayer, but one in particular caught my attention. It was the loudest amen of all, and it came from Etienne.

My Heart

Don't let anyone look down on you because you are young, but set an example for the believers in speech, in life, in love, in faith and in purity. (1 Timothy 4:12)

I was honored today. Here I am, one of the youngest ones on the show, leading the group in prayer. It just goes to show that we should never count ourselves out because we're young. God can use us all in amazing ways, at school, at church, and in our own families, even. With His strength, we can change the world.

So listen for His call. He's got great plans for us.

Good Night, God

Use us in mighty ways, Lord, even though we're young. Amen. That's my prayer. What's yours?
L8R

---

2 COMMENTS:

Stephanie said . . .
So they have a problem with you singing Christian lyrics, but they let you pray tonight? Doesn't make sense, but still pretty cool.
Posted Wednesday, 8:17 p.m.

Izzy said . . .
Well, it's mostly Marshall who has trouble with the whole Christian lyrics thing. Everyone else has been pretty cool about it.
Posted Wednesday, 11:59 p.m.

D@y 88: Normal No More

Mood Meter: System Overload

In two days it will all be over, our last songs sung, the judges' final opinions spoken, the newest *International Pop Star Challenge* winner crowned. There are times when I get teary-eyed just thinking about it. I mean, after all the excitement of the last two months, it's going to be weird waking up to normal days again. But then, there are other moments when I can't wait for this whole thing to end. I long to just hang out in my own room and be Izzy, not Izzy the pop star, but plain old Izzy Baxter. Today was one of those "I just want to be Izzy" days.

The whole day was a trip through stressville. The craziness started early, when we headed to a recording studio to record a single with the *Pop Star Challenge* top ten. The song was for a CD compilation of the show's pinnacle performances. They gave us the song a couple of days ago so we could practice, but it was hectic having to record it all in one day. Between takes, Etienne helped me out with some of the technical aspects of recording since I had never recorded at a real studio before. It felt good just talking like friends again, and his advice definitely helped. Luckily, the track is being produced by Brit star Puma, who's one of the top five producers in the world right now, so I think it will end up sounding pretty cool, despite my frazzled attitude.

When we wrapped it up over there, Atsumi and I hopped in a limo and headed to Madison Square Garden for yet another run-through of Performance Night. I guess I'm kind of glad we've been rehearsing so much, because with this much practice there's no way I'm gonna mess up. Being that tomorrow is the big show and all, you would think Werner would cut us loose early. THINK AGAIN. We rehearsed until about ten at night. Crazy!

After it was all over, I felt like falling asleep right there on the stage. But sleep wouldn't be easy, considering the news Werner casually sprang on us as we gathered our things to go. "Peoples!" he called. "Due to the extreme success we've had this season, Quest Studios has informed me that the top ten contestants will be hitting the road within the next couple of months for a ten-city world tour." Etienne, Atsumi, Miklos, and everyone else seemed excited at this information. I, on the other hand, didn't know whether to clap or to cry. Right now I'm craving LuLu's, not limousines; my cozy room, not sold-out arenas.

I just want normal, but I'm starting to think that normal is long gone.

My Heart

God is our refuge and strength, an ever-present help in trouble. Therefore we will not fear, though the earth give way and the mountains fall into the heart of the sea. (Psalm 46:1–2)

Life changes when you grow up, and I'm a bit overwhelmed about that right now. With all this pop star madness invading my life, I wonder if I'll ever be able to do little-kid things again. Will I ever be able to sit out on the fire escape or walk to church anymore without paparazzi hunting me down? Or will I constantly have to travel, record, or perform somewhere?

I guess I need to keep telling myself that even though everything has changed, God hasn't. The God who took care of me when I was a baby is the same God who is taking care of me as a teenager. "Though the earth give way and the mountains fall into the heart of the sea," I'll always be God's little girl.

Good Night, God

Lord, in this roller-coaster life, help me find peace in Your unchanging love. Amen.
That's my prayer. What's yours?
L8R

---

2 COMMENTS:

James Baxter said . . .
Get some sleep, sweetheart. Everything is going to look less
  overwhelming in the morning.
Posted Thursday, 11:23 p.m.

Pastor Ryan said . . .
Relax, Iz. You're going to rock this thing. We'll all be praying.
Posted Thursday, 11:45 p.m.

D⌀y 89: @Performance Night New York

Mood Meter: Double Berry Bliss

I can't believe it's actually over! My final performance has been signed, sealed, and delivered. Now it's all out of my hands and up to the world to decide my *International Pop Star Challenge* fate. What a relief!

The night was entirely insane, in a cool sort of way. My dad drove me to Madison Square Garden in his rental car about four hours early. After a quick prayer in the car, he gave me a hug and headed to JFK airport to pick up Anders. Yay!

From the moment I stepped foot in the arena, I was swamped. With sound checks, makeup, wardrobe, and last-minute interviews, every last second was booked. I didn't even have time to get nervous until fifteen minutes before I was supposed to go on. That's when a horrible thought dawned on me. My dad wasn't back from the airport!

Standing side stage during Atsumi's performance, I noticed the seats in the front row reserved for Anders and my dad were empty. It totally freaked me out. Here was possibly the biggest night in my life, and my family was going to miss it. When Atsumi absolutely nailed her version of "Let It Be," I was glad. The standing ovation the crowd gave her before the judges could even speak bought my dad some more time to get there.

In the middle of my desperate prayers, I felt the lights dim and heard Sean Moore announce my name. The big moment had arrived, and I was alone. As the crowd roared, I carefully walked up the backstage stairs and faced the thirty-thousand-plus crowd for the first time. As the music started, they waved their cell phones like fireflies in the darkened arena, and it was beautiful. But even more beautiful was the scene that I saw directly below. My dad, Anders, and Maddie were sitting in the front row, and next to them, in a wheelchair, sat Ms. Adelina.

With complete joy in my heart, I stepped into the spotlight and began to sing.

> *When I look into the mirror, I can't see what You can see*
> *'Cause I'm always out of place,*
> *And no camera can erase what's me.*
> *I'm so tired of acting stupid, when my heart is on the line,*
> *But every time I turn around,*
> *You keep telling me I'll do just fine.*

By the time I got to the bridge, I was oblivious to the audience. I was just a girl on a fire escape, singing out to the God she loved.

> *Now I know, I know I'm gonna make it through*
> *'Cause I feel brave, when I'm with You.*

It was smooth sailing right into the chorus, and I lifted my hands to heaven and sang like never before.

> *I can't believe, I can't believe You love me,*
> *That You're turning my failures into something lovely.*
> *Now all I really want to do is give this broken heart to You*
> *'Cause I can't believe, I can't believe You love me.*

After I was done, I stepped down these stairs at the front of the stage and just hugged my dad and brother for what seemed like forever. I don't know why, but I started crying. I think I was just relieved that it was finally over.

I felt good about my performance tonight, but I'm not so sure if it was enough to win. Oh, the audience went crazy wild, and so did Giuseppe Rossi and Aiko Mae. They were on their feet clapping for what seemed like forever. But Marshall Phillips, well, that's another story. He trashed my song choice, my voice, and even my shoes.

You know, his comments may swing a lot of votes over to Atsumi, so I guess I should be stressed about that, but I'm not. I'm actually sky-high happy. You see, I wasn't singing for the judges, or even the crowd this time around. Tonight I was performing for an audience of One, and when it was all over, I could feel His smile.

My Heart

He will take great delight in you, he will quiet you with his love, he will rejoice over you with singing. (Zephaniah 3:17)

Did you know that God cheers for us? He really does. He *delights* and *rejoices* over us. We're His children, and when we worship Him, when we love others, when we do the right thing, He's right there, cheering us on. So we should all chase after God's applause. It's the best kind.

Good Night, God

Lord, thanks for delighting and rejoicing over us. That makes me happy. Amen.

That's my prayer. What's yours?

L8R

3 COMMENTS:

Stephanie said . . .

Beyond amazing performance, Izzy. I think it was your best one yet. Can't wait till you come home.

Posted Friday, 10:07 p.m.

Maddie said . . .

In twenty-four hours, I'm gonna be best friends with the newest *International Pop Star Challenge* winner!

Posted Friday, 10:29 p.m.

Sabine said . . .

Marshall Phillips wouldn't know a pop star if he was staring one in the face, and tonight he was!!

Posted Friday, 10:54 p.m.

Day 90: @Vote Night New York

Mood Meter: Happily Ever Aftering?

I'm sitting in my hotel room, high above New York, trying to recover from my last ever *International Pop Star Challenge* show. I'd like to tell you that everyone in the world absolutely loved my performance, and that I got more votes than anyone in the history of the show. I'd like to go on to explain how the crowd went bananas when I walked onstage to pick up my recording contract and belt out my victory song. I'd like to say all of that and more, but I can't.

Well, I did get more votes than *almost* everyone in history. More people voted during this year's finals than ever before. But in the end, Atsumi was the one they called center stage during the last five minutes of tonight's show. She was the one who was given a massive recording contract by Marshall Phillips, and who joyfully got to sing one more tune on the *Pop Star* stage in front of thirty thousand screaming fans.

Of course, I'm happy for Atsumi. I tried to congratulate her backstage after the show, but I couldn't because of the tsunami of entertainment reporters crushing in on her. Yeah, there were reporters crushing in on me too, but I didn't really feel like talking, so after answering a few questions, I found my family and headed back to the hotel.

About an hour ago, when I began packing for our morning flight home, I saw my Pop Star Plan journal at the bottom of my guitar case. I gently picked it up and hugged it close like an old friend. The journal had been with me for seven years, and my eyes started to tear up as I looked at some of the crayon doodles I had drawn on the back cover way back in elementary school.

I carried it over to the bed and spent the next half hour flipping through its worn-out pages. As I read each of the plan's one hundred rules, I marveled at how far I had come. What started out as a tiny dream in a six-year-old's head had turned into reality. Incredible!

Reaching the last page, I noticed some room down at the bottom. There wasn't much space, but if I wrote small, I could get one final rule to fit. I pulled a pen out of my backpack and smiled as I wrote.

Pop Star Plan Rule #101: "Don't sing for fairy-tale fame or the approval of friends, for record deals or riches. Sing to make God smile."

2 COMMENTS:

Ms. Adelina said . . .
And that, Preciosa, is the best rule of all.
Posted Saturday, 8:24 p.m.

Izzy said . . .
NEWS FLASH, everyone! Giuseppe Rossi just called my dad. He wants to meet us in the lobby in five minutes. My dad asked him if we could meet in the morning, but he said it couldn't wait. I'll keep you posted!
Posted Saturday, 11:57 p.m.

Wow. Make sure you check out my final video blog at www.izzyspopstarplan.com/videos. And keep in touch with me online! Till next time.
·Izzy

DREAM ON
THE revolve TOUR
2011

Awesome **music**, **real-life** stories,
drama, and a ton of **fun** combine for
a **high-energy**, inspirational, encouraging
2-day weekend event for teen girls!

Appearing @Dream On

| Britt Nicole | Courtney Clark Cleveland | Chad Eastham | Group 1 Crew | Kathryn McCormick | Jamie–Grace Harper | Hawk Nelson | Jenna Lucado Bishop |

2011 Tour Dates

Garland (Dallas), TX	1/21-22	Special Events Center
Duluth (Atlanta), GA	1/28-29	Arena at Gwinnett Center
Kansas City, MO	2/4-5	Kemper Arena
Denver, CO	2/18-19	Denver Coliseum
Phoenix, AZ	2/25-26	U·S Airways Center

Portland, OR	3/4-5	Memorial Coliseum
Baltimore, MD	3/11-12	1st Mariner Arena
Lakeland, FL	3/18-19	Lakeland Event Center
Columbus, OH	3/25-26	Nationwide Arena
Hartford, CT	4/1-2	XL Center
Reading, PA	4/8-9	Sovereign Center
Ontario, CA	4/15-16	Citizens Business Bank Arena

DON'T MISS IT!
Register Today! 877.9.REVOLVE (877-973-8658)

Check out **RevolveTour.com**
then follow us here: